"Good Lord!!!" eyed, as well as placing ... her heart. Errol followed her gaze to the window, where he caught a quick glimpse of something…horrid. Ruinous, desiccated flesh clung lazily to a nightmarish, skeletal face. Small wisps of gray-white hair hung in random clumps from a dome-shaped skull that housed two lidless eyes.

It was only in the window for a second, and then the thing - some sort of ghoul - was gone, its footsteps clumping audibly as it apparently walked down the porch towards the edge of the house.

Errol grabbed his crossbow, already cocked and loaded, and raced out onto the porch. The skeletal thing was almost at the corner of the house when he fired. The bolt took it in the upper right shoulder, sinking in deep. Knocked off-balance and sent spinning by the shot, the creature fell off the porch and into the dirt.

Errol stood still, breathing heavily, with Gale behind him as the ghoul started to get up. He could now see that the bolt hadn't just gone in deep; the head had travelled all the way through and was actually sticking out of the monster's chest.

The thing reached up and gripped the arrowhead. With a grunt, it yanked the bolt out, spewing an arc of green ichor from the wound. Still holding the arrow, it began walking towards them. Belatedly, Errol recalled that he hadn't brought any more bolts outside with him (not that he would have had time to cock and load the crossbow anyway). Reaching down, he pulled his throwing knife free of its scabbard and threw it in one smooth, seamless motion.

The knife flew true, straight at the monster's throat. Almost absentmindedly, the creature batted the blade aside with the arrow it still held. The knife went into one of the porch's supporting posts with a metallic twang, vibrating.

The thing closed the distance between them in surprisingly quick fashion, so fast in fact that Errol only had time to place himself protectively between Gale and the monster before it was standing right in front of him. It thrust the arrow at Errol…

WARDEN: BOOK 1

WARDEN
Book 1: Wendigo Fever

By

Kevin Hardman

WARDEN: BOOK 1

Cover Design by Isikol

This book is published by I&H Recherche Publishing.

ISBN: 978-1-937666-08-8

Printed in the U.S.A.

WARDEN: BOOK 1

ACKNOWLEDGMENTS

I would like to thank the following for their help with this book: As always, I am thankful to GOD for all HE has done for me; my children, who keep me on my toes; and my wife, who keeps me grounded.

WARDEN: BOOK 1

WARDEN: BOOK 1

Ward /wôrd/ -

1. A division or district of a city or town, usually for administrative, representative or political purposes;

2. A person under the protection, custody or care of another;

3. A means of protection or defense; to protect or guard

Warden /wôrd'n/ - A person charged with the protection, custody or care of something

WARDEN: BOOK 1

Chapter 1

For the millionth time in his sixteen years of life, Errol Magnus decided that being a Warden had to be the absolute worst job on the planet. How could a single occupation simultaneously be the most boring, abominably stupid, *and* extraordinarily dangerous profession imaginable? And yet, here he was, staying absolutely still for what must have been hours (*boring!*), while hiding in a giant dung heap (*stupid!*) from a raging manticore (*dangerous!*). For a day that had started out so well, everything had gone horribly wrong in amazingly short order.

The day had begun with Errol's older brother Tom, in atypical fashion, allowing him to sleep in an extra hour. Being the brother of the Warden essentially meant that Errol was - unofficially - a Deputy Warden (complete with uniform!), and most mornings Tom had him up with the sun. The day usually started with exercising - primarily running and calisthenics - followed by weapons training. Breakfast would come next, and then studying. Lastly, they would make their rounds for the day.

Needless to say, Errol hated the entire routine - aside from breakfast, that is. Although he came from a long line of Wardens (including his father, his father before him, and *his* father before *him*), Errol had no intention of entering the family business. Rather than spend the rest of his life patrolling some rural, backwater ward, he hoped to eventually make his way to one of the cities (which were allegedly free of the types of beasties he and Tom currently tackled on a far-too-regular basis).

On the particular morning in question, Tom's odd behavior in giving Errol additional time to sleep should have served as an indicator that something untoward was happening. Instead, Errol had - foolishly, in retrospect - assumed his brother was starting to mellow and not take things so seriously. Other warning signs, such as Tom stating that exercise and weapons training would be skipped, were also ignored.

It wasn't until Errol was eating breakfast that Tom sprang his trap.

"A raven came in late last night," Tom had said nonchalantly. "A manticore was spotted out by the Devers' farm. I want you to track it and set the ward."

Errol, who was shoving a piece of bread into his mouth at the time, nearly choked. This was exactly the kind of thing that made him hate the whole idea of Wardens.

"Look," Tom had gone on, before Errol could voice any objection, "I know you haven't done it before with something like a manticore, but you should be beyond this stage now. I was setting wards for things like this with Dad back when I was twelve. You're four years older than I was then. It's time."

The mention of Dad, as Tom well knew, would evoke compliance from Errol. Their father had died seven years earlier saving young Jennie Bevel from a swamp constrictus. It was sad, but not unanticipated; Wardens weren't expected to live long lives. There was an old adage:

A Warden who dies of old age is said
To have allowed his charges to die in his stead.

In other words, if you live a long life as a Warden, you haven't been doing your job very well as far as protecting those in your care - your wards. As if life wasn't hard enough living this close to the Badlands.

They had left shortly after breakfast, each packing their own gear: weapons, food and water, camping items (heaven forbid, though, that they should have to spend the night outside) and more. Errol had only had time to briefly review the reference manuals on the topic of "manticores" before they left. He had wanted to take the appropriate book with him, but Tom had refused.

"You have to know this stuff," Tom had said. "If you start taking books with you they'll become a crutch, and you'll never be able to do anything without them."

Thus, the horseback ride out to the Dever farm was mostly a silent affair, with Errol trying to remember everything he could about manticores and the wards for restraining them, and Tom giving him time for reflection.

En route, they had encountered - separately - a direwolf and a gulon. In each instance, Tom had insisted that Errol ward the monsters off, which he was able to do successfully and with little effort. He had even received a rare compliment from Tom, which made Errol suspect that perhaps his brother had called the beasts in order to get Errol relaxed before having to deal with the manticore. Lots of Wardens were known for their ability to drive away monsters from the Badlands, but Tom was quite rare in having the talent to actually summon them. (Errol, however, saw little value in a skill that allowed you to beckon things that only wanted to eat you.)

Fancy Dever, the patriarch of the Dever clan, had been waiting for them when they arrived. Errol didn't know what his given name was, but everyone called him "Fancy" because - as a young man - he had always wanted to leave the farm and move to the city (to be a "fancy city boy" as everyone said). Eventually he did leave, but came home to Stanchion Ward several years later with a greatly changed mindset. He tackled farm work with aplomb afterwards and took over when his own father died.

Fancy was a fountain of knowledge about city life, but he advised Errol (and anyone else with ideas of moving there) against it. When Errol had once asked about cities being free of creatures like those in the Badlands, Fancy had merely said, "There are monsters everywhere, even in the cities. The only difference is that the ones there tend to walk around on two legs."

On this specific morning, Fancy had taken Errol and Tom to a corner of one of his fields and shown them a few large bloody splotches on the ground.

"My eldest boy, Cedric, saw it right here yesterday," Fancy had explained. "Said it swallowed one of our milk cows whole and then went trotting into the woods."

Tom had nodded sagaciously while Errol had gotten down from his horse and began removing the requisite paraphernalia from his pack. This included, among other things, his warding wand and one-hand crossbow. His dagger and throwing knife were, as always, at his left and right hip, respectively.

Properly armed (or at least as well-armed as conveniently possible), Errol had looked around for the monster's leonine tracks and began following them into the dense undergrowth nearby that marked the edge of the forest. The Badlands. Although he would never say it aloud, Errol had hoped that Tom would follow to oversee everything. To his chagrin, Tom stayed put, talking to Fancy about something mundane, like the size of this year's crops.

WARDEN: BOOK 1

The tracks were well-formed and deeply imprinted. At a guess, Errol figured the manticore would be full grown - at least ten feet in terms of body length, and more than twice that from nose to tail. He followed the tracks as stealthily as possible, relying more on the noise of wildlife - birds, insects, and the like - to give him warning should he start closing in on the creature.

As he walked, Errol mentally went through what he knew about manticores. They were fierce creatures, with the body of a lion, the tail of a scorpion, and large leathery wings like a bat. More often than not, the face of the monster would be almost human in appearance, which was quite unsettling. He was not surprised that it had eaten Fancy's cow whole, as manticores - with the ability to unhinge their jaws like serpents - had a reputation for swallowing prey in that manner. Moreover, like so many of these weirdling beasts, manticores also had a predilection for human flesh. The sting from its tail would inject its prey with a paralyzing venom, and then the poor victim would be eaten whole - clothes and all - leaving nothing behind. (Aside from, perhaps, some blood from when the prey was stung.)

About two hundred yards into the forest, Errol came to a clearing, in the center of which sat a small hill. The tracks led to the base of the hill, where there appeared to be the entrance to a large tunnel. Mounds of freshly churned dirt were scattered around the front of the tunnel. *Of course!* The manticore had dug itself a burrow.

Errol stood still and listened for a few moments. Birds in the forest canopy were chirping loudly, and other small animals on the forest floor were also making noise. He took this to mean that either the manticore was not around, or it was in the burrow and had been there long enough for the normal sounds of the forest to resume.

Deciding that it was safe for the nonce, he had circled around and crept up to the tunnel entrance from a side angle, so that anything inside would not witness his approach. Moreover, the wind was now taking his scent away from the entrance. (Manticores allegedly had terrible eyesight, but an incredible sense of smell.)

When he got close enough, he again became as still as a tree, this time listening for any sounds of life coming from within the tunnel. After a few seconds, he caught the sound of deep, rhythmic breathing. *It was asleep!*

Quickly, quietly, Errol began using his wand to etch an immobilization ward on the ground in front of the tunnel. Unless the creature was a proven man-killer, Tom's standard operating procedure was to immobilize beasts like this, and then put an impulsion ward on them to make them stay away from areas inhabited by people. If they found their way back a second time, despite the impulse put upon them, then Tom would eliminate them.

Without warning, the breathing pattern inside the tunnel changed, became a sort of snorting. Errol hastily put the final touches on the ward as a low growl rumbled forth from the dark recesses of the burrow. Satisfied, he muttered the activation incantation, causing the ward to flare light blue for a second, before quickly scrambling away. He stepped back into the brush of the forest, then circled around until he was once more in view of the tunnel mouth.

As he watched, he garnered the impression of movement inside the blackened interior of the burrow. He brought up his crossbow, with the bolt pointed directly at the entrance of the tunnel. He was so high-strung that he almost pulled the trigger the second he saw something coming from the darkness into the small patch of light at the front of the hole. He sighed in relief, relaxing and letting out a breath that he didn't know he had been holding. It was a man coming out of the tunnel. He didn't recognize the person, but the man had wide-set eyes, a broad nose, and sideburns that ran down into a thick beard.

Errol chuckled silently to himself, thinking how morosely comical it would have been if he had plugged this guy with an arrow. He was about to step into the clearing and say so when the face - and the rest of the body attached to it - moved farther into the light. Errol froze. *It was the manticore!*

Somehow, he had mistaken the monster's face for human. (However, aside from what he could now see were razor-sharp teeth and cat-like ears, it was a forgivable error.)

Errol watched in horror and fascination as the monster stepped from its lair. Because of where he had drawn the ward, the creature wouldn't be able to avoid stepping on it - even if it knew what it was. As Errol watched, the manticore's right forepaw came down on the symbol he'd drawn. Almost immediately, blue light blazed up from the ground.

In a perfect world, the manticore would have become frozen, immobilized by the ward's magic. As it was, the creature uttered an unearthly howl of pain and anger as it hopped immediately to the side. Its roar had a riptide effect, causing the surrounding forest to become instantaneously silent. As if animated by the monster's anguish, its scorpion tail whipped viciously back and forth, seeking the source of the injury, before slamming into the ground a few times with concussive force in the exact spot where the ward was drawn.

Errol knew with dread and certainty what had happened. In his haste to finish the ward, he had somehow etched the symbol incorrectly. Thus, it hadn't immobilized the beast, only wounded it in some way. Worse, instead of having a paralyzed manticore in front of him, he had one that was wounded and angry - and therefore much more dangerous.

Slowly and inconspicuously, Errol began backing farther into the dense bush of the forest. He kept his eyes on the manticore as he did so, noticing that it favored the limb that had touched the ward. The monster gingerly tested the paw, placing it on the ground and carefully putting weight on it.

Still thankful that the monster had not yet noticed him, Errol's good fortune came to an end when, through his slow, backwards retreat, he stepped on a dry twig. To Errol, the sound it made as it snapped was as loud as a thunderclap in the muted forest. Suddenly, the monster's ears perked up. It roared again, looking around as it did so - an obvious attempt to make any nearby prey flee.

It looked in Errol's direction - directly at him - and roared again, a sound full of ferocity and bloodthirst. It was all Errol could do not to run, but he remembered the creature's poor vision and knew that it couldn't see him. He merely had to be patient and wait it out. Then his luck took a final turn for the worse.

The wind subtly changed directions, and Errol now found himself upwind of the manticore. The creature had opened its mouth, presumably preparing to roar again, when it suddenly sniffed the air. It sniffed again, then looked towards Errol once more. This time, he had no doubt that it knew where he was.

The beast's brow furrowed and it bared its teeth as a low rumbling growl came from its throat. Errol saw the muscles and tendons in its legs tense as it squatted slightly before taking a powerful leap into the air. Spreading its wings, the monster was able to cover a tremendous amount of distance and was coming straight at Errol.

On his part, Errol almost soiled his pants as he suddenly had a vision of himself getting stung by that scorpion tail, and then gobbled up whole for supper. Raising his crossbow, he fired - almost out of instinct. After years of training, he was proficient enough that he should have been able to put a bolt through the manticore's eye. As it was, the shot went wide right. The creature was about halfway to him when his legs seemed to develop a mind of their own, and a few seconds later he was running helter-skelter through the forest as fast as he could go. Behind him, crashing through the underbrush with predatory snarls, came the manticore.

Errol knew the monster was close behind him, and he fought every instinct to avoid glancing back. To do so would probably cost him precious seconds, and he would need every advantage if he was to survive this encounter.

Thankfully, the density of the trees and shrubs in the woods meant that the monster couldn't use its wings. However, it was still fairly fleet on the ground, and could clear a lot of shrubbery with its leaping ability. Moreover, it had his scent, so there was little chance of shaking it off.

All of this flashed through Errol's brain as he ran, literally, for his life. Because of his training, he had great stamina - he could run for miles at a stretch - but he didn't kid himself; there was no way that he could outrun this monster. Soon, he would start to tire, slow down. Latching on to the thought unintentionally, he suddenly felt as though the manticore was right on his heels, hot breath blowing on his neck as that tail poised to strike...

Ahead of him, he saw two large boulders in close proximity to each other - maybe two feet apart. He ran for the gap between them. As he got nearer, he realized that the space between them was smaller than he thought. Nevertheless, he leaped between them, turning his body to the side as he went through and clearing the gap with barely an inch to spare on either side.

Errol hit the ground and rolled as a thunderous impact sounded behind him. He came up and glanced back. The manticore had indeed been right behind him, but had been too large to fit between the gap in the boulders. In fact, it had practically wedged itself between them. It clawed the ground ferociously, growling in frustration. For good measure, the creature's tail stabbed one of the boulders - which all of a sudden let out a blaring screech of its own and began to move. In blatant alarm, Errol suddenly realized these weren't boulders that he had squeezed through; they were trundlers!

Trundlers were creatures that seemed to be a cross between a giant pig and a mutated elephant. They grew to be the size of a small house, and - while mainly herbivorous - they were known to eat just about anything (including dirt and rocks) and would consume and void their own body weight in food several times per day.

Errol had been running so hard and so fast that he hadn't even noticed the smell. Neither had the manticore, which suddenly began squinting almost spasmodically and scratching its nose with a paw, as if there were some irritant inside that it couldn't get out.

Although still in mortal danger, Errol grinned and began looking around. *There!* A fragrant (to put it nicely) mound of manure half again as tall as he was and six times as big around. He spared a glance back at the manticore - it still appeared disconcerted by both the trundlers and the smell of their bodily wastes - then raced for the dung pile.

Errol didn't hesitate; he dove in, turned back around, and then crouched. The disturbed mound of manure, still soft and fresh, shifted and dung cascaded down around Errol, effectively covering him.

****

It was this position that Errol now found himself in as he reflected, once more, on how insane a person must be to want to be a Warden. His concentration, however, was constantly broken by the smell surrounding him, which was intense. Little wonder, then, that the manticore had seemingly lost his scent. Small slivers of light came through tiny gaps in the mound, and the darkening of these - by a body blocking the light, as well as the occasional growl - let him know when the manticore was right outside.

Thus, it seemed to Errol that hours had passed. He didn't know how patient manticores were, but he wasn't going to suffer through the indignity of becoming a human turd just to end up in some monster's gullet. He would stay there as long as he had to.

However, if he didn't end up a meal, it seemed just as likely that he would suffocate. The trundler stench was almost unbearable. Errol had tried breathing through his mouth, but that had made it feel as though he were eating the dung (a thought which nearly made him gag) rather than just hiding in it.

Just when he thought he couldn't take it anymore, the chuckling voice of his brother said, "It's okay, Errol; you can come out now. I've taken care of the manticore."

Errol was just about to move when it suddenly occurred to him that it may not be Tom. The manticore had a human face; could it mimic human voices? Certain monsters in the Badlands could. He decided to stay still.

"Come on," the voice said. "I don't plan to be out here all day. Let's go."

When Errol still didn't move, the voice continued. "Look, I followed your tracks right to this mound and they disappear. If I were the manticore - which can't copy human voices, by the way - and I knew you were in there, I'd just dig you out. Now come on. The quicker you step out, the quicker you can get cleaned up."

Still wary, Errol stayed put.

"Alright," said the voice, "you're making me pull out the big gun. When you were seven years old, Dad and I left you alone to take a bath for a few minutes. You thought we'd be gone for a while, and when we came back you were-"

"Okay!" Errol screamed, bursting from the dung heap like some hellish babe being born. "That's enough!"

Tom took one look at his younger brother and broke out into a fit of laughter. As did Fancy Dever, who was with him. Errol ignored them both and, looking around and at the sun to get his bearings, began walking in the direction of the Dever farm.

Chapter 2

Tom was still laughing as they made their way home. Errol was out of his uniform and wearing some clothes borrowed from one of Fancy's sons. After arriving back at the Dever farm, Fancy had been kind enough to let Errol take a bath in the family's tub.

"He needs to get that manure off him now," Fancy had said, "while it's still fresh. If it dries on him, he'll reek of it for weeks."

The Devers had also taken his uniform, promising to wash it thoroughly and send it to him in a few days. Finally, they had lent him the clothes he was currently wearing.

As it turned out, he hadn't been in the dung heap for hours. It was, at most, about thirty minutes.

"It's the fear," Tom said, as he had mentioned numerous times before. "It distorts your perception of time, among other things."

Tom and Fancy had come racing through the forest just as soon as they heard the manticore's howl - probably when it first stepped on the ward. They had tracked Errol and the monster to the dung heap, where Tom had immobilized the still-present manticore and then placed an impulse on it, driving it away. On their way back to the Devers', Tom had taken a moment to examine the ward Errol had etched, although he had reserved comment until now.

"Take your ward, for instance," Tom said. "It looks like you started out fine, but towards the end, it became kind of a mess. I'm not sure that would have immobilized a flea, let alone a manticore."

Errol silently fumed. He had told Tom what had happened - the whole sordid mess - and now it was lecture time. It was clear that, as the manticore started waking up in the tunnel, he had indeed panicked and screwed up the ward.

"Likewise with your crossbow shot," Tom continued. "From what you tell me, you should have been able to nail that thing with your eyes closed. Plus, you could have fired at him with your warding wand. Did you forget you had it or something?"

Errol suddenly lashed out, unable to take any more criticism. "Well, I'm sorry that everybody can't be as strong and brave as Warden Tom!"

"It's not about being brave," Tom countered. "It's about keeping your head. There's nothing wrong with being afraid; I'm afraid just about every time I come up against something from the Badlands. But you can't let the fear control you. Do that, and you're as good as dead."

"Which is exactly why 'becoming a Warden' doesn't rank very high on anyone's bucket list - especially mine!"

They rode the rest of the way home in silence.

Chapter 3

They arrived back home - at the Warden Station - late in the afternoon. Although his brother insisted that he smelled just fine, Errol was convinced that some trace of the trundler aroma still lingered. That being the case, he decided to take another bath while Tom went to check on the ravens.

As he bathed, scrubbing himself vigorously with lye soap, Errol reflected on the day's events. Everything that had happened neatly summed up the exact reasons why he thought anyone wanting to be a Warden was an idiot. *Stupid, boring, and dangerous!* If it wasn't manticores, then it was ghouls or griffins or some other kind of walking nightmare. Bearing all that in mind, it wasn't hard to believe that there had once been a time when there were no Wardens.

According to the old stories, there were other worlds out there - dark realms where all these monsters came from - that co-existed with the world of men. However, there were once strong barriers in place that kept the weirdlings on their side of the fence - although occasionally one would somehow slip through. But human beings, in their arrogance, had experimented with forces they didn't understand (and certainly couldn't control), resulting in the demolition of the walls between worlds. Monsters of every ilk, creatures that at one point were only the stuff of legend, came pouring through. Now mankind fought tooth and nail for survival on a daily basis.

In addition, men now found themselves living in a world bereft of many of the conveniences they had once taken for granted, like automobiles. (Errol, however, found it hard to believe that the rusting metal hulks that he and Tom often passed on the road had, centuries earlier, served as the primary form of transportation.) Purportedly, when the walls between the worlds collapsed, some kind of invisible force - Tom called it an EMP - had washed over the planet, causing all kinds of devices to stop functioning. Still, it was rumored that - in the cities - men were learning how to reclaim mastery over the old sciences and technologies.

All of this went through Errol's mind as he thoroughly washed his hair and attentively scrubbed almost every pore raw in an effort to convince himself that he was as clean as possible. As he stepped out of the bath and began to dry himself, he wrestled with the idea of whether or not to have another discussion with Tom about his desire to move to the city.

"Discussion" was, of course, a euphemism for a heated and angry war of words. Tom always said that Errol wasn't ready - that he had no idea of what life in a city would be like. As if Tom did. Although he had indeed taken a few such trips to various cities in the past, Tom had - for the most part - lived his entire life in Stanchion.

Theirs was a small township of about two thousand people - mostly farmers. However, many of the farms, like that of the Dever family, pushed right up to the edge of the Badlands, where all kinds of things-that-go-bump-in-the-night lurked. When Errol had been younger, he had once asked his father why people chose to live so close to the monsters as opposed to somewhere else.

"Because," his father had said, "at some point you just have to make a stand. For a long time, we let the monsters push us, make us move, give up the places we'd called home for generations. But there's only so much arable land. There's only so much potable water. We're at the point where human beings have to fight to hold on to what we have left, or we're doomed. That's why the Wardens are so important."

Errol thought lovingly of his father as he dressed, but didn't care much for his philosophy of life. Errol thought it best to reside as far away from the Badlands as possible. In his mind, the people of Stanchion (and all other similarly situated communities) should let the monsters have the farms and move on.

After getting dressed and putting on one of his spare uniforms, Errol headed to the dining room for supper. Tom was already there, waiting for him with the table set. The meal had apparently come while he was in the bath. After a short prayer by Tom, they dove into the food, which consisted of bread, cheese, and a delicious beef stew. There was even apple pie for dessert. For breakfast the next day - which was typically delivered with the evening meal - there would be bacon and biscuits.

This was about the only good thing about being a Warden: the food. In addition to a place to live and a stipend, the people in the various wards were expected to provide the food for their Wardens. Some Wardens took full advantage of this, requiring elaborate meals to be cooked for them every day.

Tom, however, followed the precedent of the previous Wardens of Stanchion. He let the people of the ward decide and rotate amongst themselves the duty of providing the food. Moreover, he didn't even demand that every meal be cooked. ("We need to know how to cook for ourselves," he'd always say when someone delivered a raw leg of mutton, a bushel of corn, or such.) His only requirements in this department were (1) that he be informed in advance whether the food being delivered would be cooked or not, and (2) that a certain amount of dry meat, cheese, salt, bread, and other nonperishable foodstuffs be delivered every week. The former item advised Tom of whether he needed to make time to cook; the latter requirement usually served as lunch when they made their daily rounds.

After finishing dinner and clearing the table, they both set about recording the day's events in their respective daily logs. It was one of the things Errol hated; having to jot down everything that happened every day just served as an additional reminder after every close encounter of how likely it was he was going to die young. Even more, he'd also have to cite it in the reference manual under "Manticore."

Complaining about it, however, would do no good. Documenting daily events was one of the many traditions Tom insisted on perpetuating. In fact, the library shelves in his office were filled with the logs of all the previous Wardens of Stanchion, as well as the reference manuals and other odd books.

"You may not realize it," Tom had said on numerous occasions, "but the information in those books has saved my life, yours - just about everybody in this town at one time or another. What we learn today can save somebody's life tomorrow."

Needless to say, Tom took his role as Warden very seriously. Although not really an inherited post, being Warden, much like other professions, was a trade that tended to be handed down from father to son. Tom had come into the job seven years ago, at age fourteen, after their father died.

It was unusual for someone so young to take on the role, and there were many who felt he was *too* young at the time. In fact, Mayor Sterillo had even written the High Warden about appointing someone new to serve in the position. All such talk came to an end when, less than a week after their father's death, Tom faced down and warded off a griffin that had killed three people before he got to it. After that, no one questioned Tom's age, abilities, or fitness, and the mayor had quickly and quietly withdrawn his request.

As usual, Tom finished logging his entry and reference citation well before Errol (who, on this occasion, was concerned with wording his log in such a way that any future reader would not consider him a buffoon.)

"I have to go out," Tom said, as Errol continued writing. "I need to go see Dorsey Carroll."

Errol's ears perked up at this. Although Tom usually allowed - actually *insisted* - that Errol accompany him on most outings and when he made his rounds, he had never allowed his younger brother to come with him to see the mysterious Dorsey Carroll. All that Errol knew about Dorsey was that he lived by himself somewhere in the Badlands (which was either brave, crazy, or both), and that Tom usually went to see him about every two weeks. It was the same routine that their late father had maintained with respect to Dorsey, which made the mystery surrounding the man that much more intriguing.

"And no, you can't come," Tom said before Errol could even ask the question.

"I didn't even say anything," Errol complained.

"You didn't have to. Now come on out to the barn so I can remind you of a few things before I go."

With that, Tom had walked out the door, with Errol trailing behind him. He listened absentmindedly as Tom ran through a litany of things to do that Errol was already aware of: fresh water for the horses, check the ravens, blah, blah, blah.

Tom appeared to already be prepared for the trip. In fact, it seemed that he hadn't unloaded a single thing from earlier; his travel kit still appeared to be fully packed. (The only additional item Errol saw was a sack of salt - something Tom always took when he went to see Dorsey.) That being the case, Tom simply swung his saddle onto a fresh horse, cinched it, and began leading the horse out of the barn. It was then that Errol noticed that he had his log with him - something that only occurred when Tom expected to be gone for an extended period of time.

"Will you be back tonight?" he asked as he closed the barn door.

"I plan on it," Tom said as he climbed into the saddle. Then he followed Errol's eyes to the log. "This is just for me to refresh my memory on a couple of things."

With that, he rode off into the fading twilight.

Chapter 4

Tom hadn't returned by the time Errol woke up the next day. It wasn't the first time that Tom had stayed away all night, so Errol saw no need to worry as he went about his daily routine.

On occasions like this, when he was left to his own devices, Errol always faced the temptation of slacking off: skipping morning exercises, weapons training, or the like. However, he recalled quite vividly how close the manticore had come to catching him the day before (not to mention his miss with the crossbow) and ultimately decided that it was best not to vary from his daily custom.

Having settled his internal debate, Errol began his day, as usual, with a run. Generations of runner Wardens had created a well-worn path around the Warden Station, which was a multi-acre property containing a number of buildings: in addition to the barn, there was a wagonshed, a grain silo, a henhouse/aviary, and several others.

The primary structure was, of course, the Station House. Not only did it contain the Warden's office, but it also served as living quarters with a kitchen, bedrooms, and so on. Errol had lived there his entire life, as had multiple generations of the Magnus family before him.

His run was followed by a quick set of calisthenics: push-ups, sit-ups, chin-ups, and more. Then it was on to weapons training.

As the descendant of Wardens (not to mention the brother of one), Errol had more than a passing familiarity with weapons. He had been handling them for as long as he could remember, although his proficiency with them really took off after Tom took over his training following their father's death.

Most Wardens were rumored to have an arsenal at their disposal, and Tom was no different. They had an abundance of various types of weapons: longswords, shortswords, daggers, longbows, crossbows, bolos, what have you. Moreover, Tom had made sure that his little brother had at least proficiency - if not mastery - of them all. To that end, Errol had to practice with at least five weapons per day.

On this morning, with the previous day's debacle still fresh in his mind, Errol decided to work with his ranged weapons. With that understanding, he set up the archery target on its usual spot on a huge oak tree out by the station's corral. Then, starting with the longbow, he practiced his shooting. As he had for the past two years, he placed all five practice arrows in the bull's-eye. Likewise with the full-sized crossbow. And the one-hand crossbow, the blowgun, and his throwing knife.

Finally, he took out his warding wand. He picked out a leaf on the oak tree, focused, and pointed the wand. A bright spark flew from it towards the leaf in question, which disintegrated upon contact with the light. He did this four more times, with four different leaves, before stopping, satisfied with his accuracy in using both conventional weapons and the mystic one.

Of course, it was easy to hit a target that was sitting still and not trying to gobble you up for dinner. Still, he recognized the truth of what Tom had said: he had panicked the day before - both in sketching the ward and in firing his crossbow. (Not to mention completely forgetting about his wand.)

After finishing with the weapons and putting them away, Errol had a light breakfast of the bacon and biscuits that had been delivered the night before, remembering to leave some for Tom. Then he turned to studying.

Of course, he had long ago mastered the rudiments of reading, writing, and arithmetic. These days he spent his time studying the various denizens of the Badlands and the wards to fend them off. Normally, Tom would have given him the topics of study (upon which Errol would be tested later), but in this instance he was left to choose his own subjects.

Of course, the very first ward he looked up was that for the manticore. Looking at it, he could see exactly where he had gone wrong in drawing the symbol - and why it had failed. He sighed despondently, noting that he had made a simple error (albeit one that almost cost him his life.) If there were a silver lining to be found, it was the fact that - like most students who miss an easy problem on an exam - he was unlikely to ever make that same mistake again.

He finished his studies (including practicing his wards) and then attacked his chores around the station. He let the horses out into the corral to graze and made sure they had fresh water. He scattered feed for the chickens before collecting eggs from the henhouse. While there, he also checked the aviary, which was in the same structure. A raven had come in - probably during the night - from the Beverly farm.

The message - as all such notes carried by birds - was brief and to the point:

TROUBLE IN FIELDS - COME

Errol crafted a short reply, stating that Tom was not present but that he'd pass along the message upon his return. He attached it to the proper bird's leg and released it. The bird would arrive at the Beverly place in short order. They hadn't identified the specific problem, so he assumed it wasn't an emergency. And even if it was, he wasn't about to attempt anything without his brother. In fact, it was with that thought in mind that Errol clung close to the Station House for the entire day, doing little or nothing besides daydreaming of life in the cities.

****

Near evening, Chad Sterillo, the mayor's son, showed up with food - a salad, sandwiches, and fried potatoes for dinner, and baked ham and bread for breakfast. He took away the pots and pans from the previous day's meal, which Errol had thoughtlessly forgotten to wash - something that Tom would undoubtedly admonish him for.

As to Tom, Errol's brother had not yet returned, which was not totally unheard of. What was unusual, however, was the fact that he hadn't sent word. Outside of one of Tom's lengthy city excursions, Errol couldn't recall a single day in the past seven years when he hadn't received some kind of communication from his brother.

Errol ate dinner in unaccustomed solitude, then made a short entry in his log before going to bed.

Chapter 5

Tom hadn't returned by the next morning, nor had he appeared by the day after that. Errol, untroubled on the first day at his brother's absence, grew increasingly worried. Tom had a reputation for being one of the most competent Wardens around, so any concern about him was probably silly. Still, Errol found himself going through his daily routine like an automaton, as anxiety over Tom gradually occupied more and more of his thoughts.

Moreover, in addition to his normal chores, he found himself forming another habit: responding to messages from the Beverlys. Each morning a new note came from them for Tom to come by their farm, and each day Errol replied that Tom was not there, but he would inform him of their request as soon as he returned. However, on the fourth morning of Tom's disappearance (for lack of a better term), there was no such message waiting for him.

This actually came as a bit of a relief to Errol. The Beverlys, like most farmers in Stanchion, were decent, hardworking folk. However, whereas the patriarch, Dennis, had a tendency to be soft-spoken and restrained, his wife was the total opposite. A mail-order bride from a far-removed province, she was not the shy and demure spouse Dennis had been promised when he paid his marital fee. She was a brash and outspoken firebrand who spoke with a weird brogue, and she could administer as severe a tongue-lashing as Errol had ever heard.

Somehow, though, this marriage of opposites had worked, producing three boys and six girls. Moreover, while the boys all seemed to inherit the gentle demeanor of their father, the girls, unfortunately, took after their mother. In short, the Beverly women were a clan of shrill harpies, and Errol had always been of the opinion that it would be the girls this time around ordering spouses, because no man with knowledge of them would willingly marry into that family. Shockingly, however, the three eldest girls had all managed to snare local grooms, a turn of events that Errol attributed to the fact that the Beverly women never took "no" for an answer.

Thus, it should have come as no great surprise to him that - around dusk of that fourth day - a horse and rider came trotting determinedly up the path to the Station House just as he was about to have dinner. The dining table actually sat in front of a window that gave a clear view of the path approaching the house. Although the sun was setting fast, there was still enough light left for him to make out that the rider was female, wearing a light blue blouse and brown trousers. As she got closer, he could see that she had red hair, a telltale indicator that the rider was one of the Beverly girls.

Not good, Errol thought, suddenly all too aware of how his messages had probably been received by the Beverlys.

The rider stopped her horse at the front porch and swung out of the saddle with practiced ease. It was Gale, one of the middle daughters (although the eldest still at home since her older sisters had married). At seventeen, she was a year older than Errol and rather tall for a girl - just a few inches shy of Errol's own six-foot frame - with a shapely figure and clear, smooth skin. The fiery red of her hair (another thing inherited from her mother) was offset by the calm, clear blue of her eyes. All in all, she would have been quite pretty - perhaps even beautiful - if her features were not permanently marked by a perpetual scowl.

Surprisingly, that scowl was not on her face as she burst into the room, without knocking, like a tempest in search of something to destroy.

"Good evening," she said, smiling sweetly as she closed the door. "I take it the Warden still hasn't returned yet?"

Errol, in the midst of raising his fork to his mouth, paused to answer. "No, not yet. Like I said, I'll tell him to come as soon as he gets back." He then went back to eating, barely sparing Gale a glance.

"Well, I'm sorry," she said apologetically. "I see now that I've obviously interrupted your supper. What exactly are you having this evening?"

"Chicken in broth," he responded irritably, "with wild rice and bread."

"Sounds delicious," she said. Then, without warning, she leaned forward and snatched the plate off the table.

"Hey!" Errol screamed, jumping up. Gale, paying him no mind, turned around and opened the door - and flung the plate outside into the dirt.

"Are you crazy???!!" Errol exploded. "What the hell is wrong with you???!!!"

"Me?!" Gale retorted, slamming the door shut. "You're the one sitting there gorging yourself like a hog instead of doing your duty!"

"What duty? I'm not the Warden. Riding out to your farm is Tom's job, not mine."

"Not your job? Well, you sure do act like it's your job when it suits you."

"What's that supposed to mean?"

"It means that you live in the house *built* for the Warden. You ride horses *provided* for the Warden. You eat the food *cooked* for the Warden. It sounds like you want all of the perks of the job but none of the responsibility."

Her words stung Errol somewhat. He had never considered the possibility that people would actually want *him* taking action when Tom wasn't around. The ramifications shocked him.

"So," Gale continued, "if you aren't going to take the post seriously, you should move on to something else, and the people of this town can go to supporting a single person at this Station House - cooking for just one, providing necessities for just one...Good Lord!!!"

Her sudden change of tone snapped Errol out of his reverie. Gale had gone pale and bug-eyed, as well as placing a hand over her heart. Errol followed her gaze to the window, where he caught a quick glimpse of something...horrid. Ruinous, desiccated flesh clung lazily to a nightmarish, skeletal face. Small wisps of gray-white hair hung in random clumps from a dome-shaped skull that housed two lidless eyes.

It was only in the window for a second, and then the...thing...was gone, its footsteps clumping audibly as it apparently walked down the porch towards the edge of the house.

Barely wasting a second, Errol grabbed his crossbow, already cocked and loaded, and raced out onto the porch. The skeletal thing was almost at the corner of the house when he fired. The bolt took it in the upper right shoulder, sinking in deep. The momentum of the shot also spun the creature around, knocking it off-balance and causing it to fall off the porch and into the dirt.

Errol stood still, breathing heavily, with Gale behind him. When she made a move to step forward, he instinctively put out his arm to keep her back. All the while, he never took his eyes off the creature, which sat up and then calmly came to its feet before turning towards them. Errol could now see that the bolt hadn't just gone in deep; the head had travelled all the way through to the other side and was actually sticking out of the monster's chest.

The thing reached up with a gloved hand and gripped the arrowhead. With a grunt, it yanked the bolt out, spewing an arc of green ichor from the wound. Still gripping the arrow, it began walking towards them.

Belatedly, Errol recalled that he hadn't brought any more bolts outside with him (not that he would have had time to cock and load the crossbow anyway). Reaching down, he pulled his throwing knife free of its sheath and threw it in one smooth, seamless motion.

The knife flew true, straight at the monster's throat. Almost absentmindedly, the creature batted the blade aside with the arrow it still held. The knife went into one of the porch's supporting posts with a metallic twang, vibrating.

The thing closed the distance between them in surprisingly quick fashion, so fast in fact that Errol only had time to place himself protectively between Gale and the monster before it was standing right in front of him. It thrust the arrow out to Errol.

"You need to be more careful with this thing, boy," it said nonchalantly. "You could have killed somebody."

Chapter 6

Warily, Errol took back his arrow.

"Uh...thanks," he muttered unsurely. Now that it was closer, he saw that the thing was actually dressed like a human. It wore boots, black pants, a white shirt with a vest, and a full-length black duster. It also wore gloves and a hat.

"What is that thing?" Gale asked urgently, still behind him.

"Some kind of ghoul, I guess," Errol said over his shoulder, afraid to take his eyes off the monster.

"Actually, I'm a zombie," the creature interjected.

"Aren't they the same thing?" Gale asked.

"A common misconception," the zombie said, laughing. "A ghoul is a living creature that eats human flesh. A zombie is a deceased person who has been reanimated through some means - black magic, in my case."

"Black magic?" Errol muttered, going back on the defensive. Bringing a corpse back to life by black magic was rarely ever done for a *good* reason.

"Never fear," the zombie chuckled. "My master, the magician who brought me back, was killed by a Warden - your grandfather, in fact. With his death, I became free, and no longer subject to his evil will."

"You knew my grandfather?" asked Errol incredulously.

"Forgive me," the zombie said, extending a hand. "I'm Dorsey Carroll. I should have introduced myself at first, but I guess I was distracted - getting shot with a crossbow will do that to you."

"Wait," Errol said, confused but shaking the proffered hand. "You're Dorsey Carroll? My brother's friend? My *father's* friend?"

"Yes, although now you can see why they never made any introductions. And why I never come into town." He chuckled again.

"So what are you doing here?" Gale asked.

"Tom was supposed to come see me the other night. He never showed."

"Hold on," Errol said, suddenly concerned. "Tom never made it to your place?"

"No, that's why I'm here. Tom's never been a no-show before. I came to see if something had happened to him."

"Any chance we could take this conversation inside?" Gale asked, cutting off Errol's next question.

"Fine with me," Dorsey said, then walked inside without waiting for any further invitation. Gale and Errol followed, and all three settled down at the dining table.

"What do you think could have happened to him?" Errol asked.

The zombie shrugged. "Hard to say. It's the Badlands; anything could happen. I mean, there's all kinds of magic and mayhem that goes on out there. Back during your grandfather's time, there was a guy who went hunting one day and disappeared. Twenty years later, he walked out of the woods, looking like not a single day had passed. Moreover, he swore he'd only been gone a few hours."

"What happened to him?" Gale asked.

"He had trouble readjusting," Dorsey said. "Lots of friends and relatives had died while he was gone; his kids were all grown and didn't know him. In the end, he just walked back out into the Badlands and disappeared again - this time, for good."

Errol asked the obvious question. "Could something like that have happened to Tom?"

"Possibly," Dorsey answered, "but I doubt it. Tom knows the Badlands too well, knows what can happen. There's very little out there that he can't handle. Now that I think about it, I'd give it a few more days before I started to worry."

"Here's an idea," Gale said, as Errol reflected on Dorsey's comments. "Why don't you take three or four days to search the area near where Dorsey lives?"

"What about the problem you're having in your fields?" Errol asked.

"Don't worry about it," she answered, pooh-poohing the notion with a wave of her hand. "It won't kill us to have to deal with it for a little bit longer."

Errol contemplated the idea. In truth, Tom would have hated it. In Tom's mind, the people he protected came first. He would probably go into conniptions if he knew that Errol was willing to put off the needs of the community to search for his older brother. In the end, Errol settled on a compromise.

"I'll tell you what," Errol stated, "I'll give it two days. If I don't find him by then, I'll come by your farm to deal with your issue, and then go on with the search."

That seemed agreeable to Gale. At this juncture, Dorsey cleared his throat.

"Well, if that's settled," the zombie announced, "I'll be getting back to my place. I assume, Errol, that you'll be coming with me." Following Errol's nod, the zombie continued, "Then there's just one other thing. I have certain, uh, dietary restrictions, which is the thing that Tom usually helps me with."

"What exactly do you need?" Errol asked guardedly, unsure of the response he'd get.

"Salt."

WARDEN: BOOK 1

Chapter 7

Errol was packed and ready to go in short order. For food, he took about four days' worth of dried meat, biscuits, and cheese. (He also pulled a sack of salt from the pantry for Dorsey, as it was apparently a very important part of the zombie's sustenance, although he didn't explain how.) For weapons, he took along his mainstays: the one-hand crossbow, his warding wand, his throwing knife, and his dagger. He also brought his axe and his staff, although the former was primarily for chopping firewood should he have to spend the night outdoors.

Finally, almost on a whim, he decided to take the miniature blowgun. It was a small weapon - the entire thing could almost be hidden in his hand - and the tiny darts it fired were far from lethal. However, having been dipped in a paralytic ointment, the darts did occasionally come in handy.

As soon as he was ready, he and Dorsey got under way - the former on horseback and the latter on foot. (Dorsey, being undead, apparently had a great deal of stamina and could walk at a rather fast clip almost indefinitely. Moreover, horses found his presence unnerving to a certain extent, so he couldn't have ridden anyway.) Despite a full moon, it was still too dark to see very much unaided. Thankfully, after uttering the proper incantation, the end of Errol's warding wand glowed with bright luminescence.

Gale, it had been decided, would spend the night at the Station House (after, of course, sending a raven with a message to that effect to her family's farm). Errol felt bad that she had to stay there by herself and that he didn't have time to escort her home, but there was very little chance of anything happening to her. In uncharacteristic fashion, she had given him a hug before he left, and two words: "Be safe."

****

Two days of searching blazed by amazingly fast. Using Dorsey's small cabin as a base, Errol had searched the surrounding area in exceptional detail and found no trace of his brother. No campfire, no latrine…not even a hoofprint from his horse.

Unfortunately, he had his promise of visiting the Beverly farm to fulfill, so on the third morning he reluctantly packed up and prepared to leave. As he climbed up into the saddle, he extended his hand towards Dorsey, who was seeing him off.

"Thanks for your help," Errol said.

"No problem. Your family's been helping me for decades now." Errol smiled at that as Dorsey continued. "One last piece of advice. Keep your eyes and ears open more than usual."

"Why's that?" Errol asked, frowning.

"I don't know exactly. Just a feeling. Being undead, I'm attuned to certain forces, and the past few days I've been starting to get an odd feeling, like something new and malevolent has arrived."

"Does it have anything to do with Tom?"

"From the feeling I've been getting, I hope not. I hope, wish, and pray not, because I'm not sure that even Tom could stand against whatever this thing is."

Chapter 8

Errol gave serious thought to Dorsey's words as he made the trek to the Beverly farm - a trip that would take almost the entire day. The Badlands were dangerous enough at the best of times, and even that was putting it mildly. The thought of some new peril adding to what already existed kept him on his toes for the first few hours of the journey, although he encountered nothing more than minor weirdlings that he was easily able to ward off.

Around midday, he noticed smoke rising above the trees. *A campfire!* Assuming that it might be Tom, he headed towards it, only to be disappointed when he arrived.

He didn't even have to get down from his horse to see that this was someone else's camp. First of all, although he didn't see anyone, he saw their gear spread around, and none of it was his brother's. In addition, their equipment appeared to have been tossed about willy-nilly; Tom kept things well-organized at his campsites.

Errol sighed in disappointment and prepared to leave, when it occurred to him that the camper might need assistance. Looking down at the ground, he could track where it appeared someone had gone off into the underbrush.

"Hello?" he called out, loudly and clearly, in the direction of the tracks. His voice echoed slightly through the trees. He waited a few minutes, then called out again. This time, a nearby voice answered in response.

"Hello? Who's there?" someone - a male - called out.

Errol squinted, looking into the dense shrubbery and saw a darkened form moving towards him. He checked to make sure his crossbow was ready and held it inconspicuously at his side as he answered.

"My name's Errol Magnus. I was just checking to see if everything was alright."

"Everything's fine," the voice answered, and a large man stepped from the woods into the campsite. He was tall and rather rotund, but Errol got the distinct impression that his portliness consisted of more muscle than fat. Obviously middle-aged, he had salt-and-pepper hair that ran neatly down into a matching moustache and beard.

He carried a broadsword in a scabbard at his side. Around his neck he wore multiple necklaces made of various metals - gold and silver among them - as well as bracelets on his wrists and armbands inscribed with odd symbols. Finally, numerous tattoos covered almost every patch of visible skin except his face. All in all, his was as curious an appearance as Errol had ever seen.

"Forgive me for not answering immediately," the man said, "but I was…indisposed. My name is Jarruse."

He extended a hand, which Errol shook before asking, "What are you doing out here?"

"Gathering herbs, my young friend. I'm an apothecary. I make medicines, elixirs, and such."

"You do know you're in the Badlands, right? That all kinds of things live out here, and a lot of them consider human beings a delicacy?"

Jarruse smiled at that. "I'm aware, but much of what I need only grows here. I had hired a group of guards to accompany me, but they deserted me in the middle of the night after receiving their pay. I don't have the funds to pay again, so it was either continue alone, or go back and face economic ruin."

"Hmmm," Errol groaned. "If I had a business that required me to go into the Badlands, I'd give serious thought to doing something else."

"That's a surprising point of view coming from a Warden."

"*Deputy* Warden," Errol corrected. His profession (to the extent it could be called such for him) wasn't difficult to guess; the all-black uniform - black shirt, black trousers, black boots, black hat - was a dead giveaway. "My brother Tom is the actual Warden for this region."

Jarruse frowned. "Did you say 'Tom'?"

"Yes," Errol answered, his interest now piqued. "Do you know him?"

"Well, I met him."

"When? Where?"

"Maybe a week ago, not too far from here. It was at night - some of the herbs I use only bloom in darkness - and he was headed to see a friend, he said."

"What happened?"

"Well, I saw that he was a Warden, and I told him about my men deserting me. I also told him about some weird creature I'd seen the previous night."

"What kind of creature?"

"I don't know," Jarruse said in agitation. "Just something big and probably dangerous. It was dark and I only saw it for a few seconds, moving through the trees, growling. And it walked on two legs."

"Two legs?" Errol was surprised. Only a handful of weirdlings were bipedal, although a number of them - like dogs, cats, and other domesticated animals - could rear up on two legs when it suited them.

"Anyway, he went to investigate."

"And…?"

"And what? That's it. I didn't go with him, so that's the last I saw of him."

Errol groaned in frustration as he swung down out of his saddle. He opened up his saddlebag and removed a map, then asked Jarruse to try to pinpoint the area where he'd seen Tom and the direction he'd pointed him in.

Chapter 9

Errol rode the rest of the way to the Beverly farm at high speed, getting there shortly before sundown. No wonder he hadn't found any traces of Tom around Dorsey's place; Tom had never even gotten close. Instead, the course he had most likely travelled - towards Jarruse's sighting of the mysterious creature - had taken him in a different direction altogether.

Upon arrival, Errol was all business, barely greeting Dennis and his wife before asking to be escorted to the problem area in the fields. (And asking for a fresh horse, since his own was completely worn out.) Not surprisingly, it was Gale who came with him, riding silently on her own horse as Errol brought her up to speed on what he had found out about Tom.

"So that's good news, then," she said when he'd finished.

"Good as far as me knowing where he went. Bad when you consider the fact that I haven't heard from him."

Both chewed on that in silence as they came to an open area in the cornfield. Looking around, Errol could see that the stalks in a long, but relatively narrow streak had wilted, shriveling up into hard, dry husks. He climbed down from his horse to have a closer look, with Gale doing the same.

"Looks like some sort of blight," he said. "What makes you think you need a Warden for this?"

"Because, when we look out here at night, we see something big and glowing moving around, and the next morning there's more damage."

"At night?" Errol looked in sudden alarm towards the horizon, where the sun was now setting.

"*Later* at night," Gale stressed, while getting a lamp from her pack and lighting it. "Nothing's ever happened this early."

Errol nodded, poking a digit into a small hole in the ground, about the width of his forefinger. He looked at her and grinned. "Come with me for a second."

With that, he moved over to where the healthy cornstalks were still growing. With Gale peering over his shoulder, he hunted around until he found what he was looking for - another small hole in the ground like what he had previously observed. He pulled out his warding wand, and drew an intricate symbol on the ground around the hole. When he finished, he muttered a small incantation and the symbol glowed bright yellow.

"What are you doing?" Gale asked.

"Shhhh," he replied, putting a finger to his lips. "Watch."

As the glow began to fade, a small amount of activity seemed to take place in the hole. There was an impression of movement within, and tiny bits of earth around the surface edge crumbled inwards. Suddenly, there was a high-pitched squeak and something green popped up out of the hole so quickly that Gale and Errol both were taken aback.

When they recovered, they saw what appeared to be a little man - a child, really - no taller than a man's thumb straddling the tiny hole. He was dressed in a tiny green wrap that appeared to be made of the leafy husk of an ear of corn.

The little man squeaked again and pointed at the two humans. Errol quickly etched another ward on the ground and activated it. However, the expected glow - this time blue - did not completely fade from this one.

"What is that?" Gale asked.

"A Perrikin. They live underground, usually in cultivated fields, so they can get food from what people plant."

"And it lives here?"

"*They* do. They live in colonies - probably all across your farm."

"Can you get rid of them?"

Errol looked at her, surprised. "Why would you want to do that?"

"You just said they steal our crops, our food. They're like any other pest."

"No, they're not. They actually help you. They clip the diseased portions off plants, help the roots stay healthy, take care of them. Your farm probably hasn't had a bad harvest in what - six, seven years?"

"More like ten."

"Well, this is probably why. And they don't take very much - you guys probably never even notice it's missing. Or you just chalk it up to some other pest taking it."

Again, the little man squeaked, and suddenly the symbols on the new ward moved, eerily changing shape.

"He wants to know what we want," Errol said.

"You can understand him?" Gale asked in surprise.

"Not exactly. This last emblem I sketched is a translation ward. The symbols tell each of us what the other is saying."

"Can you tell us about the dead crops?" Errol asked. "We want to fix them."

Suddenly, as the translation ward changed, the little man became extremely excited, jumping high into the air (for him), clapping his hands and pointing to the blighted cornstalks, all the while chirping incessantly.

"He says, 'The Riser! The Riser! The Riser!' - whatever that means," Errol translated. "He just keeps saying it over and over."

Suddenly the little man jumped back into the hole feet-first and disappeared.

"Well, that was rude," said Gale. "Not even a goodbye."

Before Errol could reply, they heard squeaking and chirping behind them. Turning around, they saw the little Perrikin standing above another small hole in the area of the wilted cornstalks. He motioned intently for them to come over.

"Guess he wants to show us something," Errol said as he and Gale walked to where the Perrikin was standing. However, when they got close, he jumped back into the hole, only to pop up a few feet farther down the lane of wilted plants.

"I think he wants us to follow him," Gale said.

They again approached the little man and again he disappeared, appearing above ground a few feet away. This pattern repeated itself several more times until they reached the end of the area with the blighted crops. This time, when they got close, the Perrikin didn't disappear. Instead, he jumped up and down excitedly, pointing at the ground.

"Here?" Errol asked, looking at the area that their guide was indicating. Upon closer inspection, he saw that the earth in the designated area actually rose up into a slight mound.

Looking at the ground, Errol had a bad feeling, but Gale asked the question he was actually thinking.

"Is that...is-is something buried there?" she asked.

"Only one way to find out," Errol responded.

With that, he took out his dagger and started scraping clumps of dirt off the top of the mound. Fortunately, the ground was still loose, and in very little time he had unearthed what was clearly a human body. It was dressed in ragged, bloody clothes and lay face down in the dirt. Its dark, stringy hair was matted with dried blood. Around the right wrist was a bracelet of silver links with a single dark gemstone set in the center. Errol couldn't see the face, but from what he could observe of the body and the style of dress, it wasn't anyone who he was familiar with.

He turned to Gale. "Anyone you know?"

Gale, a little pale, simply shook her head in the negative.

"Well," Errol continued, "I think–"

He was cut off as the Perrikin began its excited squeaking again, then jumped back into its hole. They looked around, waiting for it to pop up again, but it didn't. Errol was wondering what to make of it all when a gasp from Gale drew his attention back to the body. It was moving.

"I guess we know what our little friend was trying to tell us just now," he said, as the body got up on its hands and knees. Errol put out an arm to draw Gale back behind him, thinking this was the second time in their last two meetings that he had put himself between her and potential danger. With his other hand, he drew his wand and held it up defensively.

The body came slowly to its feet, surrounded by an eldritch glow. Nearby crops began to wither, indicating that this thing was definitely the source of the blight.

"Is this what you think you've been seeing in the fields?" Errol asked. He felt rather than heard Gale nodding behind him.

"I thought you said it only appeared *later* at night!" he hissed.

"I did, but nobody was out here poking it with a knife then."

Errol was on the verge of making a sarcastic reply when the body turned in their direction and appeared to look at them. He couldn't exactly tell, though, because the thing's eyes were completely blood-red. The front of its shirt was open, and Errol almost gasped at what he saw. Whatever this thing was, it had once been human - a man; however, monstrous damage had been done to its body. It appeared as though some fierce predator had taken an immense bite out of its chest - Errol could see the clear white of bone in the light of Gale's lamp. Likewise, its stomach had been ripped open, and its intestines and internal organs trailed to the ground like sausages and meat hanging in a butcher's window.

"Death," the creature said, and took a step towards them, raising its claw-like hands. "Revenge."

Gale screamed. Errol held out his warding wand and uttered a word of power. A bright spark of light shot away from the tip of the wand towards the creature. Gore splattered as the light struck the thing, but it barely slowed its advance. Errol hastily drew a defensive ward in the air, which then shimmered with light as he uttered an incantation.

The thing moved again towards them, but suddenly seemed to bump into an invisible barrier.

"Death!" it said again, more fiercely this time. "Revenge!" Its hands beat against the invisible wall.

Errol breathed a sigh of relief. For a second, he had been worried that he would mess up the ward - drawing them in the air was harder than etching them on something you can see, like the ground, but just as effective (although they wouldn't last long if not activated right away).

"What is that?" Gale asked, as the creature continued to feel around the unseen barrier, trying to find a way around it. "Is it a zombie, like Dorsey?"

"I don't think so," Errol answered. He watched as the creature continued muttering the same two words - "Death!" and "Revenge!" - as it found itself boxed in on all four sides by invisible forces. "I think it's a revenant."

"What's that?"

"A corpse or a spirit that was somehow wronged in life - usually betrayed or murdered - so it comes back seeking vengeance. Notice how it keeps saying the same two words?"

Gale nodded. "Yes, but we haven't betrayed or killed anyone. Why is it here?"

Errol shrugged. "Revenants often have unusual abilities. It's probably materialized on your farm because something here is connected to its need for revenge."

"So what are you going to do, blast it again with your wand?"

"No. That didn't do much good last time."

"It looked like it caused some damage. Just keep blasting it over and over until it's all gone."

Errol sighed in exasperation. "That may not even work, and I'm not about to wear myself out trying."

Gale was nonplussed. "Wear yourself out…?"

"Yes. The wards and the magic that you saw me do are powered by my life force, not the wand. Just like you might have to stop and catch your breath after running a long distance, I'll exhaust myself and need a breather if I do too much."

"So why do you even need the wand?"

"Why do you use a plow on your fields instead of digging them up by hand? Because the plow makes it easier. But the plow can't do anything on its own; it takes you - or an animal like a plow horse - exerting your own energy to make it work. It's the same with the wand. It's designed to make warding easier, but I don't actually need it. See?"

He lifted his right hand, palm up. It started to glow with power as a small spark - much like the one that had hit the revenant earlier - began to form.

Gale nodded in understanding as the spark and light around Errol's hand faded. "Well, if you aren't going to blast it, what *are* you going to do?"

Errol had been wondering that himself. The obvious solution lay in the answer to another question: What would Tom do?

Bulking up his courage, Errol shouted to get the revenant's attention. "Hey! Over here!"

The revenant turned towards him. "Death! Revenge!"

"Yes," Errol answered. "I know you were wronged, but you're harming innocents."

"Death! Revenge!"

"I understand that, but–"

"Death! Revenge!"

Errol sighed. Revenants were perversely single-minded in their quests for vengeance; it was essentially the only thought they knew, the only thing that drove them, and this particular specimen was a clear adherent to the rule. Errol decided on a different tack.

"Who has harmed you?"

The creature had seemingly been on the verge of uttering its full two-word vocabulary again, but then froze, mouth open.

"Who has harmed you?" Errol asked again.

The creature's brow furrowed, and its jaw worked in silence, as if mining for words that would not come out.

"Who do you seek revenge on?"

"Ma-ma-magician!" the revenant finally blurted out. "Eeeeee-vil magician!"

"Well, there's no magician here," Errol stated, sweeping his arm to take in the entire farm. "Your vengeance lies elsewhere. You need to leave this region."

"You-you would hinder?" the thing said with a snarl.

"No," Errol quickly interjected. Revenants often arose with weird powers, and the last thing he wanted was to get on this one's bad side. "But your presence here is a disturbance. You need to move on."

"Yes," Gale spoke up, "so if there's anything we can do…"

"You will help?" it asked, almost in surprise.

"Of course! We both will," Gale answered before Errol could stop her. However, she immediately realized she had done something wrong when her response was met with a sharp intake of breath by Errol, who turned to her with a look that managed to convey a plethora of emotions, including shock, fright, amazement, and - most of all - fury.

"So be it," the revenant said. It closed its eyes, and the eldritch light covering it began to fade. At the same time, its body turned pale, ashen. Then it began to crumble as the clothes it wore, in similar manner, began to wither away. Within a few moments, nothing was left but a mound of dust.

Errol was about to speak when the revenant's remains began to move. The dust twitched, then crumbled as something rose up from beneath it. It was the creature's silver bracelet. It floated towards them and then came to a halt right in front of Errol, who took it reluctantly. He looked at the gemstone, which glistened brightly in the lamplight, then shoved it into his pocket. Then he turned on Gale.

"You stupid, stupid idiot!" he screamed. "What did you do that for?!"

Gale, getting a taste of her own medicine for once, was taken aback. "What do you mean?"

"You *never* make a deal with a spirit - especially one like a revenant, which you obviously know nothing about!"

"What deal? I just told it that we'd help it if we could."

"No, you actually agreed to help it, with no conditions."

"So, what does that mean?"

"It means that we have to help it get its revenge."

"What happens if we don't or can't?"

"I'm guessing the revenant would consider that a kind of betrayal. It'll kill us."

Chapter 10

Errol spent the night with the Beverlys, sleeping out in their barn. He slept fitfully, his dreams preoccupied with visions of Tom dead, and himself killed by a revenant. Even worse, Gale somehow managed to escape death in his dreams - something that would have been a just reward for her idiotic behavior in the real world - which made the nightmare all the worse.

He was packed and ready to go early. In his opinion, the problem in their fields was resolved, and he had informed Dennis Beverly of this the previous night when he and Gale had returned from their excursion. Although he had mentioned the revenant and its disappearance, he had left out the part about Gale's promise of help (for which she silently mouthed "Thank you" as Errol told his tale).

The family had seemed impressed with the job he'd done. Even Dennis' wife had, for the first time Errol could recall, gone an entire quarter-hour the night before without saying anything negative after he finished telling what had happened. She had even politely asked to see the revenant's bracelet. Errol didn't know how he would deal with the revenant itself, but the important thing now was to get back out into the Badlands and find Tom.

Unfortunately, the Beverlys would not let him leave without having breakfast. It was a delicious meal of bacon and eggs, which he washed down with water. Most of the family ate with him, but he couldn't help but notice that Gale was not among them. It astonished him that he would be bothered (and disappointed) by this, especially after her boneheaded antics in the field.

That being the case, he was quite surprised when, as he climbed up on his horse, she came out of the barn with her own steed saddled and ready to go.

"I'm coming with you," she stated in a matter-of-fact tone. He was about to protest when she continued. "If Tom's injured, you may need help getting him back. I can assist with that, as well as with other things."

He opened his mouth to say something - to tell her "No" - but the words wouldn't come out. He knew that this was, at least in part, an attempt to make up for the debacle with the revenant. He also remembered times when he himself had sought opportunities with Tom to make up for stupid mistakes.

"Suit yourself," he said, and then urged his horse on. He ignored the slight smile on Gale's face as her horse fell into step beside his.

****

The first part of their trip was fairly uneventful. Errol pushed the pace, but not to the extent that it would wear the horses out. He was concerned about his brother, but after this much time he knew that Tom would either be okay, or…

Gale, like most of the farmers, had never really gone any great distance into the Badlands. It would be an eye-opening trip for her, Errol knew - and hopefully one she'd live to tell about. Even experienced people like Wardens weren't assured of coming back unscathed from any trip into the Badlands - or even coming back at all.

They stopped for lunch around midday. Gale's mother had packed an ample supply of food, for which they were both grateful, since the length of this excursion was currently indefinite.

Reflecting on Gale's mother, Errol suddenly remembered that he had forgotten to retrieve the revenant's bracelet from her. Therefore, he was rather shocked to find it in his pack as he was putting things away after lunch.

"Holy..." he said, startled.

"What is it?" Gale asked with concern.

Errol held up the bracelet. "I could have sworn that I'd left this with your mother."

"Maybe she packed it up for you."

Errol shook his head. "No, I've had my pack with me constantly since we left. I think..." His voice trailed off and he stared into the distance, thinking furiously.

"What?" Gale asked after a few moments.

"I think we're tagged," he said. "The revenant's marked us. This bracelet...we can't lose it. I think it's a soulgate, with the essence of the revenant inside. It's bonded to us, marks us like familiars. It'll be with us wherever we go - until we find the revenant's killer, or *it* kills *us*."

As Gale took a moment to absorb this, Errol angrily shoved the bracelet into his pack. Unfortunately, one of its silver links caught on the pack's buckle and with the force of the push from his hand the links parted, falling onto the ground. Errol was left holding only the gemstone that was the centerpiece of the bracelet. Groaning in frustration, he thrust the gemstone into his pack, then methodically picked up the links and put them in his pocket. He didn't know what this meant with respect to the revenant, but he was sure they would find out. They finished packing and resumed their journey.

****

Towards the end of the first day, the dense undergrowth of the forest gave way to lush grass as Errol and Gale found themselves at the top of a hill. From that vantage point, they could see miles in almost all directions.

"It's beautiful," Gale said, watching the wind whip the tall grass back and forth.

"Dangerous is a better description," Errol corrected. "Remember, we're deep into the Badlands here. Anything can happen."

He looked off into the direction where they were headed, and saw small dots circling in the sky, like gnats buzzing around a discarded piece of fruit. The sight made Errol's stomach flip.

"That's where we're headed," he said, pointing, trying desperately to keep the emotion out of his voice. "It'll be dark soon so we'll set up camp now. We should get there sometime tomorrow."

Gale squinted in the direction he was pointing. "What are those things in the sky?"

"Carrion birds."

Chapter 11

For once in his life, morning couldn't come fast enough for Errol. He had carefully warded their campsite the night before, then had a quick dinner and tried to get some shuteye. However, with the carrion birds occupying a great deal of his thoughts, sleep had been hard to come by. There would be some kind of body where those birds were congregated, and when he finally did fall asleep, his dreams had been filled with scenes of vultures and crows rabidly pecking at Tom's corpse.

Gale seemed more refreshed by her night's slumber and - as Errol had to admit - was ready to travel even before he was. This was as much time as he'd spent in her presence and he was surprised to find her to actually be pleasant company. Talking with her kept him from thinking about what they were likely to find when they reached the location of the carrion birds.

****

It was shortly after midday when they arrived at their destination. Even without the birds flying above, it would have been hard to miss. First of all, there was a boisterous commotion as they drew near - an utterly disharmonious blend of sound from not just a variety of birds but also other scavengers on the ground.

In addition, there was also the smell. Gale wrinkled her nose as the scent of rot and decay - negligible at first - grew stronger as they travelled. By the time they actually came into sight of the place where they were headed, the smell was pervasive but, thankfully, not overpowering. What was staggering, however, was the scene in front of them.

They had just crested a modest hill, and saw below them a small enclosed plain comprising several acres. In the center of it stood a dilapidated wooden cabin. Throughout the acreage around the cabin, however, were numerous clumps of scavengers - some birds, some animals - attacking what had to be bodies. And there were, apparently, a lot of them.

"Oh my!" Gale gasped.

"Come on," Errol said, edging his horse forward. He gripped his warding wand in the same hand that held the reins, and had his crossbow cocked and loaded in the other.

They went forward slowly, headed towards the cabin, knowing that something was wickedly wrong here. As they came near one of the places where the feeding frenzy was occurring, the animals and birds scattered. Looking at what they had been devouring, Errol was shocked to see a dismembered leg.

However, his surprise was compounded when a second group of scavengers fled at their approach, revealing that they had been gnawing on another limb - this time an arm. A sudden realization dawned on both Errol and Gale at the same time as they looked around at the other packs of animals busy eating.

"I think," Gale began, barely able to catch her breath, "I think they're all...they're all body parts."

Errol just nodded as they continued forward. However, the closer they got to the cabin, the more skittish the horses became. The big animals began neighing in distress, their large eyes rolling around in fear.

Finally, about thirty feet from the cabin, they refused to go any farther and even reared up in revolt.

"Something in that cabin has them spooked," Errol said.

"Yeah, well, it's got me spooked, too," Gale commented.

It was clear that the horses were going to bolt once they let go of the reins, and there was no place to tie them up. That being the case, Errol held out his warding wand and put an impulse on them to stay put until he and Gale returned.

That done, they warily approached the cabin with Errol in the lead. There was a window facing the direction they were coming from, but any glass it had once held had long ago been knocked out. The door to the place was closed.

"Hello?" Errol called out as they approached. In response, he thought he heard a distorted voice and a muffled knock.

When he got close enough, he knocked on the door and called out another greeting.

"Hello? Anybody home?" he asked.

The door swung open as he rapped, and the stench of death and decay wafted out. They had thought the smell outside was bad, but the inside - being an enclosed area - was ten times worse.

And despite the smell, despite what they had witnessed outside, they were still not fully prepared for what they saw when they stepped into the cabin's interior. The place was a charnel house; there were body parts in various stages of decay strewn all around. An arm here, a head there, a torso…blood and gore were all over the floor and walls. Flies and various insects buzzed incessantly, and one bloated carcass constantly writhed with maggots crawling underneath the skin. *And this is just the first room*, Errol thought.

Gale placed a hand over her mouth, then ran outside and retched. Simultaneous with the sound of her stomach emptying its contents, Errol again heard a muffled cry, coming from what appeared to be an adjoining room.

Gale was still outside, recovering, as he stepped into the next room - trying unsuccessfully to avoid stepping in blood - and saw something he was never likely to forget. The room was empty, save for a gigantic pot in the center. It was at least five feet high, about eight feet in diameter, and covered with a massive lid. The muffled sound was coming from inside the pot, and this time was accompanied by a slight knocking.

The creak of a floorboard behind him made Errol jump. He spun, aiming the crossbow - and would have killed Gale had he pulled the trigger.

"Easy," she said, holding her hands up defensively. "It's just me."

Before he could respond, a sound - almost a whimpering - came from inside the pot again. Errol couldn't make out words, but he was pretty sure that there was a human being inside. Anxious that it might be Tom, he set his crossbow down on the floor and tucked his wand through his belt.

"Here," he said, moving around to the other side of the pot. "Help me get this lid off."

Now on opposite sides of the pot, he and Gale struggled to lift the lid for several minutes. Their efforts, however, were futile. Moreover, it sounded like the person inside the pot was starting to cry.

"Let's try something else," Gale finally said in an exhausted tone. "Let's get on the same side and see if we can angle it just enough for whoever's in there to get out."

Errol came around to Gale's side, and together they pushed up on the lid. At first it seemed stuck, but then it slowly rose. As it cleared the top edge of the pot, they pushed it over to one side so that it tilted in towards the pot's interior. It wasn't completely off, but it was tilted enough that someone inside could probably squeeze out - provided they were of moderate girth.

Unsurprisingly, the smell coming from inside the pot was worse than anything they had thus encountered. They didn't have to look inside to know that it was filled with body parts.

"Help me!" a desperate voice wheezed from inside the pot, and a skinny hand came up over the edge. Errol grabbed it and pulled, heedless of the smell (and the nauseous fluids coating it). As he pulled, he saw that the hand was attached to a scrawny little man with a scraggly beard and a crazy gleam in his eye. Moreover, he was indeed crying as he came out of the pot.

"Thankyouthankyouthankyou!" the man shouted fervently, gripping Errol's hand like a vise and trying to kiss it.

Errol freed his hand with more than a little effort. The little man then moved towards Gale, arms open in an apparent attempt to give her a hug. Errol, however, grabbed the man's shirt, which was absolutely disgusting.

"Don't worry about thanking her," he said. "You thanked me enough for us both."

The man looked confused, like he didn't understand what Errol had just said.

59

"Can you tell us what happened here?" Gale asked.

The man suddenly screeched, going bug-eyed and putting his fist in his mouth.

"Oh! Oh! Oh!" he finally said. "We have to go! Quickly! Before *it* gets back!" He scrambled towards the door - and into the first room - in a mad dash, and then outside, with Errol and Gale close behind him. Once outdoors, he put his hands up to his eyes, blinking madly in the bright sunlight.

"How long have you been in that pot?" Errol asked.

The man didn't answer. He just kept his hand up to block the sun and started mumbling to himself. Errol asked a few more questions, but could get no response other than an occasional word about needing to leave.

Finally, Gale interjected. "Errol, he's terrified. You're not going to be able to get anything out of him while he's like this. Maybe if we get him away from here - away from whoever put him in that pot…"

The words hit Errol like a lightning bolt. Something had put this man in the pot! Something that ripped people apart! Something that *ate* them!

"Quick, to the horses!" Errol shouted.

Gale grabbed the man's hand and began dragging him; Errol was right behind them when he remembered his crossbow. He shouted to Gale that he needed a minute as he ran back inside to get it.

With Gale's words still in his head, he stealthily walked into the second room. His crossbow was still on the floor where he had left it. He picked it up, glad to see that their hasty exit had not damaged it. Then he did the other thing he needed to do: he peeked over the edge of the pot.

Using his wand for light, he looked at the multitude of bodies and body parts stuffed inside. With a sigh of relief, he drew back a few moments later. He knew that in death people could take on an appearance quite different than what they had exhibited in life. Still, he was sure that nobody in the pot was Tom. (Plus, none of the body parts, to the extent they were clothed, were wearing any piece of a Warden's uniform.)

As he prepared to leave, he looked around the room for what seemed like the first time, and noticed that there was actually a window that faced the area behind the cabin. Overtaken by curiosity, he went over to it and peeked out.

He saw a sight that was already etched in his brain: scavengers picking over human remains. He sighed despondently and looked down at the ground right outside - and saw a couple of doors set in a wooden frame that appeared to lead under the house. More importantly, he saw something else that immediately made almost everything else he'd seen since coming across the cabin secondary. He raced back through the front room and out of the cabin. He heard Gale call to him, but he ignored her, running full steam to the back of the structure.

When he got there, he checked the doors closely to make sure he was right. This was obviously the entrance to some kind of storage or root cellar. However, clearly standing out on one of the doors was what he had come back here to see: a bloody bootprint. Tom's, in fact.

Tom had been here, without a doubt. Almost without hesitation, Errol tried the cellar doors and found them unlocked. He pulled them both open, revealing a rickety set of wooden stairs leading down into darkness. Again using the light from his wand, Errol went down the stairs.

There was still a stench here, but not as bad as the pot. The cellar seemed to consist of one large chamber that was surprisingly chilly; as expected, there was blood and body parts here as well, although most of the limbs had been picked clean of flesh, and the blood was less prevalent.

Thankfully, none of the bodies here were Tom. Having assured himself of that fact, Errol was so anxious to leave that he almost missed it.

He had turned to leave when the light from his wand fell over an ugly, misshapen section of wall. Lying on the floor next to it was an object he recognized. It had spots of blood on it, but without a doubt he knew what it was: Tom's pack. He raced over and picked it up. He was so excited that he almost opened it then and there, except something else caught his attention: the wall moved.

It was only a slight up-and-down motion, but it was enough to send Errol stumbling backwards. Looking carefully now, he saw that what he had mistaken for a part of the wall was actually some monstrosity. It was lying on its side, apparently asleep, facing the true wall of the cellar; the movement Errol had witnessed was actually the expansion of its chest and diaphragm as it breathed.

It was shaped like a man, but extraordinarily huge. Errol estimated it to be at least ten feet tall. He could only see one of its arms, but it ended in a hand accentuated by terrible-looking claws, as did its feet. The massive, round head was completely hairless, and - now that he noticed it - the chill in the basement seemed to emanate from this monster.

Without making a sound, Errol slowly headed towards the stairs, heedless of the fact that he was stepping in blood along the way. When he reached the stairs, he turned to look at the creature one last time - and saw that its head had turned away from the wall and it was staring at him with sickly yellow eyes.

With the need for stealth gone, Errol raced up the stairs. Once outside, he pivoted and immediately swung the cellar doors shut. One of the doors, ill-fit for its frame, bounced back up, reverberating. Errol raised his foot and stomped on the door, hard, forcing it closed and leaving his own bloody boot print superimposed on his brother's.

He raced around to the front of the house, screaming for Gale to go. Already seated on her own horse with the little man behind her, Gale took off. Almost without breaking stride, Errol leaped into the saddle of his own horse and raced behind her.

Chapter 12

They rode at top speed for the next hour, with Errol continually ignoring Gale's questions, until she insisted that they come to a stop. Her horse, burdened with two people, was exhausted and needed a rest. Errol's own mount wasn't in much better shape.

The place where they chose to stop was fortuitously located near a stream. There, they insisted that the little man take some time to bathe himself and wash the charnel stink out of his clothes. The man, however, whose name was finally revealed to be Digby, was terrified of being alone. He insisted that they stay within eyeshot of him while he took the requisite bath. (Thankfully, he only meant that he wanted to be able to see them at all times, not that *they* needed to see *him*.)

Errol took the opportunity to go through Tom's pack while Gale broke out lunch. There were, of course, the usual items, such as a nesting kit for meals and medical supplies. There was also Tom's log, which he had taken with him the last time Errol saw him. Finally, there was a weird book that Errol had never seen before.

The book was bound in some strange, leathery material he wasn't familiar with, and had unusual runes drawn on the outside of it. However, he only needed to flip through a couple of pages before he recognized it for what it was - a book of magic!

Of course, the Wardens had their own books, in which were recorded certain types of magic, such as the wards that they used. This book, however, was something entirely different. He had no idea how Tom had come across it, but he quickly put it away.

Errol then turned his attention to Tom's log. As he had hoped, Tom had jotted down other entries since the last time they were together, and Errol eagerly read them, hoping to find out his brother's fate.

What he read chilled him to the bone. He now knew why Tom hadn't come home, knew why he hadn't been able to get word to Errol. Moreover, he knew that even someone as competent as Tom might not have survived the events detailed in the log. It also explained what Errol had seen in the cabin cellar.

Tom had crossed paths with a Wendigo.

Chapter 13

"A what?" Gale asked again.

"A Wendigo," Errol repeated softly. He was trying to keep his voice down; Digby was still bathing, but Errol was afraid that mention of the thing that had captured him would further unhinge the man.

"It was supposedly a man at one time," Errol went on, "who was cursed for committing cannibalism and transformed into a monster that craves human flesh."

"Is there any kind of monster that *doesn't* crave human flesh?" Gale asked rhetorically. "Anyway, we should be safe now, right?"

Errol shook his head. "You don't understand. Once a Wendigo starts tracking someone as prey, it never gives up. It will pursue them forever if it has to. Moreover, when it catches them, it'll kill anyone with them. That's why Tom never came home. It would have tracked him there and killed him *and* me."

"Wouldn't both of you guys have been able to kill it? Ambush it or something?"

"It's not some dumb animal that's just going to walk into a trap. It used to be a man and still has the intelligence and cunning of one. On top of that, Wendigos are incredibly fast, preternaturally strong, and have enhanced senses, like hearing and smell."

"But it has to have some kind of weakness."

"Just two," Errol said, frowning. "Fire and silver. But even if you could manage to kill it, Wendigos are supposed to be able to resurrect themselves. Then they come after the person who killed them."

"So, basically this thing is unstoppable?"

Errol just shrugged. "Hopefully Tom noted some things that could help us."

With that, he went back to reading Tom's log again, which didn't describe the Wendigo itself in great detail, just how Tom had encountered it. Apparently the Wendigo was the thing Jarruse had seen, although why it hadn't come after the apothecary was a mystery. Going in the direction Jarruse had indicated, Tom had come across the cabin (and the slaughter therein), which seemed to be the monster's lair. It was also the place where he'd found the odd book of magic, although Tom hadn't been able to glean much more about it than Errol.

He read the last few entries in the log two more times before snapping the book shut and putting it away. In the last entry, Tom noted how he was starting to hear strange sounds all the time. Errol didn't want to think about what that meant, nor did he want to dwell on the fact that there were bloodstains on his brother's pack.

"Anything in there that could help us?" Gale asked.

"Maybe. According to his log, Tom's plan was to head to the fire marsh. We should do that as well."

"The fire marsh?" Gale was obviously a little shocked. "Isn't that, well, dangerous?"

"Yes, it's dangerous. So is being here. So is sneaking into the Wendigo's lair. So is farming next to the Badlands. It's all dangerous, Gale! Everything we do is dangerous!"

Gale looked at him with watery eyes, although no tears fell. He hadn't meant to let his emotions get the best of him like that, to lash out at her in that way, but she didn't seem to have an appreciation for the gravity of their situation. He had no doubt the Wendigo would be coming after them. Moreover, he still had no idea about the fate of his brother.

In truth, hers was a fair question. The fire marsh was a large boggy region of noxious fumes and combustible gases. During the day it exuded mind-boggling heat, and spontaneous fires were not unknown. In addition, it was home to a number of fierce creatures, large and small, that had somehow adapted to – and in some cases adopted – the fiery temperament of their environment.

"Look," Errol said in a calmer voice. "It *is* dangerous, but fire is one of the few things that can hurt a Wendigo. It will probably circle around if it really wants us, so going to the marsh will probably buy us some time."

"What makes you think that we'll even get that far if this monster is as strong and fast as you say?"

"Because it likes to hunt its victims, terrify them, before it kills and eats them. The fun will be over if it kills us right now. I think that's the only reason I – and probably Tom before me – ever got out of that cabin cellar alive. I think that's the only reason it left Digby alive."

"What do you mean?"

"It uses that pot to store food for a rainy day, but it put Digby in there essentially unhurt. I think it was for future entertainment value. If and when it got bored, it could let him 'escape' and then hunt him down."

Gale's eyes went wide as the truth suddenly occurred to her. "That's why you're so sure it's coming after us. This is Digby's escape. Maybe not the way that thing intended, but an escape nonetheless."

"Yes, and now we're part of the fun."

Chapter 14

After Digby finished his much-needed bath, they were back in the saddle again, with Digby eating lunch as they rode. Errol estimated that, riding a little faster than usual, they would arrive at the fire marsh the following afternoon.

They rode in solitude for the most part – or rather, Errol and Gale did. Digby, however, seemed a bundle of nervous energy, and he chattered away aimlessly about almost anything and everything. In a very short time, his travelling companions knew almost his entire life story. The only subject he tended to avoid was that of the cabin where they had found him, but eventually – in bits and pieces – they learned what had happened.

In brief, Digby had been part of a hunting expedition that had had the misfortune to encounter the Wendigo. Getting him to disclose the details had been difficult, but in essence the monster had begun showing up every night wherever they made camp. It would seemingly appear out of nowhere, moving so fast that it couldn't be seen; one second there would be nothing there, and the next it was in their midst. Blades and arrows would damage it, but the wounds healed almost immediately. Then, it would either grab one of the hunters and drag him screaming from the camp, or – more likely – would simply go away. In those instances, however, one of their band would always be missing the next morning when they woke up.

It was the same routine every night until Digby was the only person left. However, although the creature had slaughtered his companions, it took him back to its lair and placed him in the pot.

Aside from the Wendigo, Digby freely spoke about all other topics, even when it was clear that his companions were not listening. As the day wore on, however, his tireless rambling gave way to another behavior. Still riding behind Gale on her horse, he began speaking less and less and looking around, erratically, more and more. Occasionally, he would excitedly ask, "Did you hear that?" or "Do you smell that?" By the time Errol called a halt for the day, near sundown, Digby was as wild-eyed and distressed as when they had first found him.

The place where they had stopped was a previously-used campsite with several tree stumps in close proximity that could be used as stools. After warding the camp and getting a campfire going, Errol plopped down on one of them and took a swig from his water canteen. He offered some to Digby, but the man's hands shook so badly that he spilled more than he drank. Moreover, he jumped at almost every sound – even when he was addressed directly by Errol or Gale.

"What's wrong with him?" Gale asked in frustration, sitting on a stump next to Errol and out of earshot of their companion. She had just tapped Digby on the shoulder to offer him something to eat, and the man had leaped aside, screaming.

"Wendigo Fever," Errol replied.

Gale was suddenly alarmed. "What is that? Is it contagious?"

"It's less of an actual disease and more of a curse. The Wendigo's prey starts sensing things – seeing, hearing, and smelling stuff – that no one else can. They might also have nightmares that make them wake up screaming, or even physical pain, like they're on fire. Basically, they go crazy and end up running off into the woods and are never seen again."

Gale was amazed at his breadth of knowledge on the subject. "How do you know all this stuff?"

"Studying. Tom thinks a Warden needs to know everything that could be out here in the Badlands, so he makes me bone up on this kind of stuff all the time. And he tests me on it."

"I guess it's a good thing he did, because it's certainly coming in handy."

Errol silently agreed. He had never really had an appreciation for all of the stuff that Tom had made him learn, trained him to do. But now, he could see the benefit of it. Tom had done his best to make Errol a survivor more than anything else.

"So," Gale continued, "are you this knowledgeable about everything dangerous in these parts?"

"Not everything," Errol said, shaking his head and laughing. "Hardly anything, in my opinion."

"Just Wendigos and revenants, I take it."

"Well, the Wendigo thing is just kind of a fluke. Tom once asked me to name what I felt were the ten most dangerous things in the Badlands. Then he made me learn everything I could about them, his logic being that if I knew how to handle what I felt was most dangerous – basically, the things I feared the most – then I shouldn't have problems with anything else. Wendigos, of course, were on my list."

"You don't seem to be acting like you're afraid of it."

"Oh, I'm actually terrified. But Tom always says that being afraid is natural. Panicking, however, will get you killed. So I'm just trying not to panic and lose my head."

Then he told her about the manticore. How he had bungled the ward. How he had missed with the crossbow. How he was determined not to let that happen again.

****

The darkness of nightfall saw Digby's agitation grow even worse. Errol and Gale, who had sleeping bags, each offered him a blanket, as the night had suddenly turned chill. Nevertheless, the man's teeth chattered uncontrollably, and he had taken to making odd noises – short screeches and cries for no reason at all. Thus it was that Errol paid him almost no mind when Digby's latest shriek reached his ears. However, the sudden, wild neighing of the horses did capture his attention, and when he turned to see what had disturbed them, he saw it. The Wendigo was standing on the other side of their fire, just outside the periphery of their camp - and the wards.

Standing, it seemed even bigger than it had in the cellar – at least twelve feet tall. Pale white and humanoid in appearance, it was gaunt beyond belief, its ribs easily distinguishable beneath the skin of its uncovered torso. It appeared to be grinning, showing a mouth full of razor-sharp fangs and teeth, at which point Errol realized that the monster had no lips. The claws at the end of its hands clicked together spasmodically as its fearsome yellow eyes locked with Errol's own.

Not unnaturally, Gale screamed, and the Wendigo turned its baleful glare upon her. Taking advantage of the monster's distraction, Errol whipped his warding wand out of his belt and fired a spark of light at it. It struck the Wendigo in the chest, causing massive damage in the form of a fist-sized hole in the general vicinity of where the creature's heart should be.

The Wendigo absorbed the assault almost nonchalantly, the only indication that it had been hit being a slight step backwards. It casually looked down at the wound, which began to heal almost immediately.

Errol fired another spark from his wand, but suddenly the Wendigo wasn't there anymore, and the spark passed harmlessly through the place where it had been. Errol looked around warily, but the monster seemed to have left them for good. He glanced at the other members of his party. Digby was looking at the place where the Wendigo had stood, whimpering; Gale had her eyes closed and was trembling slightly.

"Gale, are you okay?" Errol asked, going to her. She nodded vigorously, not quite able to speak yet.

Errol could have kicked himself. How could he have not realized what was going to happen? Digby had mentioned that the thing had visited his camp every night. He should have realized the exact same pattern was going to repeat.

He was so lost in his own thoughts that he almost didn't see Digby starting to walk out of the camp. The man had a weird look in his eye, almost as if he were seeing something else besides the forest - something visible only to him.

Errol quickly stepped to him and grabbed the man's arm. Digby turned to him with a blank expression on his face.

"I have to go," Digby said. He tried to turn and continue walking into the woods. Errol pulled on his arm and turned him back around.

"Digby!" he shouted, then shook him.

Digby blinked, then shook his head as if to clear it. "I'm sorry," he said. "What were we talking about?"

"We were discussing how we all need a good night's sleep," Errol replied. "Right, Gale?"

"R-r-right," Gale answered, still appearing shaken. She looked like she was about to add something, when an unexpected voice sounded from nearby.

"Help me!" It was a woman's voice, filled with terror. "Someone please help me!"

Errol spun around, trying to pinpoint the source of the cries. The voice seemed to be coming from several different directions.

"Oh, no!" Gale wailed. "Someone's out there! That *thing* has them!"

She made a move as if to run in the direction of the last shriek, but Errol grabbed her arm.

"No!" he firmly shouted. "There's no one out there. It's the Wendigo." Gale gave him a bewildered look, so he went on. "It can mimic human voices. It's trying to draw us out."

With that, they tried to ignore the pleas for help, which changed over the course of the next hour to that of a young child and then a crying baby. Twice during that time, they also had to keep a blank-eyed Digby from wandering off. When Errol finally fell asleep, his dreams

74

were filled with images of bodies torn asunder and blood covering everything he could see.

****

Errol woke up well before dawn to the sound of a bloodcurdling scream. His wand was immediately in his hand. He looked and saw that Gale was also wide awake, having bolted straight up. Digby was nowhere to be seen. The scream came again, and this time something in the inflection or tone told him that it was their new friend out there, meeting his fate.

Sleep was a long time coming after that, but Errol used the time wisely. The rudiments of a potential strategy were beginning to take shape in his mind, and by the time he fell asleep again, he had the vague outlines of a plan of action for the next day.

Chapter 15

They found Digby the next morning – or rather, what was left of him – as their journey to the fire marsh continued. His corpse was about one hundred feet from where they had made camp and set deliberately along the path they were travelling so that they were sure to come across it. Like what they had discovered at the cabin, the body had been ripped apart (in fact, the head was nowhere to be found), but enough clothing remained on the body for them to recognize who it was.

Gale trembled slightly at what she saw, and tears started rolling down her cheeks.

"Don't," Errol gently admonished her, then put a hand up to his mouth as he coughed. "This was intentionally left here for us to find. It wants us scared, to know what's coming. Let's go." He coughed again.

"Sh-shouldn't we bury him? Isn't that the decent thing to do?"

"It is, but we aren't going to," Errol said, coughing once more. "It'll take time that we don't have. That's what the Wendigo wants." With that, they moved along.

****

They kept up a healthy pace throughout the morning, although travelling in almost complete silence. Outside of the ordinary noise of the forest, the only sound to be heard was the continual hack of Errol's coughing, which seemed to grow more frequent throughout the day. When Gale asked him if he was coming down with something, he simply waved her off.

They stopped only once, to refill their canteens – and anything else that would hold water – at a spring that ran close to the direction they were headed. They also let the horses drink their fill, as this would likely be their last chance at fresh water before they entered the fire marsh.

By mid-afternoon, they had reached the fire marsh itself. The first indication was the grass, previously lush and green around them, slowly giving way to blades that were brown, dry, and brittle. The trees changed as well, going from the normal, fruit- and nut-bearing variety to twisted, mutated giants with heat-resistant bark and leaves. The ground on the road ahead of them shimmered in the heat of their new environment, and as they entered the marsh proper it became soft, muddy earth that made squishing sounds as their mounts lifted their hooves out of the muck.

Errol and Gale began to sweat profusely due to the increased heat. Strange creatures of varying descriptions scuttled out of their path as they rode, occasionally spitting out noxious fumes or even fire when feeling threatened. At one point, a huge tentacle – covered with snapping maws full of knife-like teeth and with a huge, bulbous eye on top – arose from the marsh and snatched up a crablike critter right in front of them, squeezing it tight enough to crack its thick shell in seconds; the tentacle also took a swipe at their horses, but disappeared, shrieking, after Errol put a crossbow bolt through its eye. In addition, plumes of flames shot up sporadically from the ground around them – once so close that Errol's horse reared up and almost threw him.

"Doesn't walking here hurt the horses' hooves?" Gale asked at one point.

"The marsh ground isn't exceptionally hot," he answered, between coughs. "Gases and vapors float up from underground, but they don't mix and become combustible until they hit the air. Even then, they have to mix in the right combination, so while they do heat up – and keep the temperature around here blazing hot – the danger of them actually igniting isn't that great. That's why you can even build a fire in the marsh without a lot of worries, although there's still an element of risk."

Errol realized that he was talking a lot, but he was doing it intentionally. Since entering the marsh, he had noticed Gale starting to imitate some of Digby's prior behavior: looking around erratically and beginning to start at every little noise.

Suddenly she turned to him. "Did you hear that?"

"No," Errol said, then coughed again. "I didn't hear anything."

****

The Wendigo watched the boy and girl as they travelled. It was relatively far away, but had greatly enhanced vision, as well as hearing and speed. Having eaten relatively recently, it could – for the moment – ignore its never-ending, all-consuming hunger and enjoy this hunt.

The prey, it knew, sought the protection of the fire marsh. Thus, they knew something of the Wendigo's nature, its weaknesses. However, while it might avoid the marsh by day, they had made an error in presuming the same was true at night. Its stomach rumbled in anticipation at the thought of the meal they would make.

Like the little man the night before, the girl was succumbing to the Fever. The Wendigo could see her eccentric movements; it listened to her fearful questions about sounds only she could hear. Soon, its scent would overtake her as well. Before long – maybe tonight, but certainly by the next – she would come and offer herself.

As to the boy, he intrigued the monster. Although the boy appeared to be getting sick, spending the day coughing, the Wendigo had reasons for saving him for last. First of all, the boy warded, like the prey from several nights back. (The thought of that prey brought a snarl from the Wendigo.) The boy also dressed like that prey, and even smelled a lot like him. He would be delectable.

****

They stopped for the evening at the first and only patch of solid ground they managed to come across. It was obviously a well-used campsite, as Errol noted the remains of numerous campfires all around when he warded the area. Using his axe, he cut down several reedy plants from the nearby marsh that he knew would make a good fire.

As night came on, Errol's cough continued unabated. When she wasn't glancing around nervously, Gale looked at him with clear anxiety. Errol knew that she was concerned about him being sick. He was more concerned about her, because in addition to hearing things, she had now started asking him if he smelled something funny.

He built a big roaring campfire, as the marsh became surprisingly cool with the setting of the sun. Not being particularly hungry, he only nibbled at a biscuit but took a big gulp of water from his canteen before pouring some in a bowl for the horses. He was just fixing the feedbag around his horse's head when he heard Gale draw in a sharp breath.

Turning in her direction, he saw her glance at him, then point to the edge of the campsite. Peering into the darkness, he saw something move, gently bobbing from side to side. Something about it seemed familiar…

"Wait here," he instructed Gale, and then he went to investigate. A few moments later he came back grinning, holding a plant that appeared to have a little balloon on the end of it that bobbed up and down.

"It's a marsh floater," he said in response to her unasked question, then followed it with a cough. "The upper part of the plant is an elastic seed pod that's filled with inert gas. When the weather gets hot, the gas expands, inflating the pod and making it float. Some of them must be retaining a little bit of warmth from the heat of the day."

He began walking towards their campfire and, after coughing again, continued. "When it gets hot enough, the pod will break away from the rest of the plant and float away." He stopped a few feet from the fire and then slowly, carefully extended the plant towards it. The little balloon grew bigger as it got closer to the flames; then, with a small tearing sound, it broke away and floated up into the night sky.

"The hotter the temperature gets, the bigger the seed pod gets. Finally, it pops, spreading seeds all over, and that's how the plant propagates." As he finished, the floater he had released, still rising, vanished from their sight.

Errol realized he had been talking excessively, but it was partly intentional, as before. He had to keep Gale's mind preoccupied, and talking about the floaters seemed to do so, as she was still watching the spot where the balloon had disappeared. As he reflected on the fact that the effect would probably be short-lived, an idea flashed through his brain.

Errol ran back to the marsh, appearing again a few moments later with about a dozen of the seed pods – minus the plant – in his hands. Making sure he kept an appropriate distance from the campfire, he sat down on the ground and pulled out his throwing knife. In his other hand he held one of the seed pods.

Uninflated, the seed pod appeared more cylindrical than round, and was about the length of his hand. As Gale watched, Errol used the tip of his knife blade to make tiny little holes in a straight line down the length of the seed pod. Then he carefully walked towards their campfire and placed the pod on the ground with the little holes facing the flames.

The pod began expanding almost immediately, but as it did there came a small hissing sound, like air being blown through a straw. At the same time, the flames of their campfire suddenly roared higher.

"It worked!" Errol shouted, laughing. "It worked!" He grabbed another seed pod.

Gale looked on, frowning for a second, before she, too, realized what had happened.

"I get it!" she uttered, smiling. "The heat makes the gas expand; as it expands, it comes out through the holes you made. Then it hits the fire, making it burn brighter."

"Exactly!"

"I want to try!" She snatched the seed pod Errol had been holding and tossed it towards the campfire.

"No! Wait–" That was as far as Errol got before a loud *BOOM* sounded and he found himself bombarded with marsh floater seeds that hit his hands and face with stinging force.

"What happened?" Gale asked.

"I hadn't punched any holes in that seed pod you grabbed," Errol responded, wiping seeds off his face, "and you tossed it directly into the fire. Apparently, it exploded."

Gale, who had also been peppered with seeds, started giggling. Errol, although initially miffed at her, found the laughter infectious and was soon chuckling himself.

They were still smiling a few moments later when a blanket of cold settled on them out of nowhere, and the campfire suddenly shrank down low. Errol was in the process of placing about half of his supply of seed pods in his pack when it happened, and he spun around in alarm. As with the previous night, the horses appeared to go crazy, and Errol quickly saw the reason why. The Wendigo was back.

Again, it appeared on the opposite side of the campfire from him, at the very edge of the area where light from the flames reached. It seemed to watch Errol, who raised his hand to cover a cough, with great interest. Then it turned its head towards Gale, who stood off to Errol's left and appeared mesmerized by the monster. It was the opportunity Errol had been waiting for.

He raised his hand to his mouth again, apparently preparing to cough once more, but this time he held the mini-blowgun in his hand. He took a deep breath, aimed, and blew.

The Wendigo, focused on Gale and seemingly unthreatened by Errol's movements, was caught unaware when the tiny dart struck it in the abdomen. Based on its size, the dart should have been little more than a pinprick, but suddenly there was a gaping wound in the monster's belly.

The Wendigo screamed in pain, a shriek of madness and fury that was almost agonizing to hear. At the same time, a freezing wind swept across their camp, almost causing the fire to die out. The Wendigo vanished, and a second later Errol found himself hoisted well off the ground, face to face with the creature while held in its powerful grip.

The wards around the camp flared up, giving off a ghostly light. The Wendigo's skin turned red in various places, blistered and split. The monster disregarded whatever pain it felt. The wards were obviously hurting it, but not doing nearly enough damage to be effective.

Errol struggled, kicking madly and beating at the hand that held him. The Wendigo ignored him. With its free hand, it reached inside the hole in its stomach and rooted around, grunting with the effort. Then it seemed to find what it was looking for.

It brought up the object of its search – a small, oval-shaped piece of metal that glinted in the moonlight. The Wendigo held the metal up between itself and Errol in order to get a good look at it. Errol, however, already knew what it was: a silver link from the bracelet of the revenant. The metal hissed and smoked in the Wendigo's hand, scorching the monster's flesh before finally being flung away.

The idea had come to Errol the night before, and he had surreptitiously fitted one of the silver links over the end of one of his darts. Then – knowing that the Wendigo was probably watching them - he had spent the day feigning the onset of a cough, so that the movement of his hand to his mouth would be routine by the time the creature showed up at their camp.

"Clever, boy," the Wendigo acknowledged, its voice a deep, unnatural rumbling. Its breath, hot and rancid, washed over Errol's face, making him want to gag. "Now, I return the favor."

It raked the claws on its free hand across Errol's chest and abdomen. His clothing parted like water and he screamed in unimaginable agony as the thing's touch both singed his flesh with unbearable heat and - at the same time - burned it with mind-numbing cold. He fell to the earth like a limp, wet rag as the Wendigo let him drop and then disappeared.

It was another five minutes before he found the strength to stand. On her part, Gale looked to be completely in a daze the entire time.

"Do you smell that?" she asked.

Chapter 16

Following the Wendigo's departure (and the return of his strength), Errol had worked on treating his wounds. Oddly enough, despite the intense pain he had felt, the wounds were primarily superficial: three long but fairly shallow scratches that angled down in parallel lines from the upper left side of his chest to the right side of his stomach.

Of course, the monster hadn't been trying to seriously hurt him. That would ruin the hunt. Moreover, with the silver extracted, it was surely back in top form – Errol had seen the creature's wound starting to heal before it dropped him.

As to his own injuries, Errol first applied a salve from his medicine kit to fight infection. Then he took out a small tube containing a dark liquid and removed the cap from it. The tube contained an epoxy – a resin from a medicinal tree in the Badlands that would help seal the wounds even better than sewing them shut.

After applying the epoxy to the lacerations, he took his extra blanket and cut several strips from it, intending to bind the wounds. As he worked on his injuries, his mind reflected on this latest encounter with the Wendigo.

It hadn't been a bad plan, his idea about the coughing and the silver. If nothing else, it showed that the Wendigo had weaknesses and could be outmaneuvered. The trick then, was not to overpower it but to outsmart it.

It was too bad that the marsh didn't offer as much protection as he had hoped – at least not at night; it would have been great to have some additional space between them and the Wendigo, as well as more time to come up with some other tactic to try to use on the monster. Errol also regretted that he hadn't been able to tell Gale about his plan with the silver, but he was gravely concerned about the Wendigo's legendary hearing ability. That aside, it still appeared to be the right decision, because – looking at her now – Gale was obviously becoming unbalanced.

She stood in the same spot she had when the Wendigo had appeared, muttering to herself and wringing her hands. She had a completely forlorn look upon her face. When Errol called to her, it was if she didn't hear him. Errol walked over and slapped her – not hard enough to really hurt her, but with enough force to get her attention. That seemed to momentarily bring her back to herself. Within fifteen minutes, however, she was back to muttering, speaking of sights, sounds, and smells that Errol was oblivious to.

Errol sat her down on her sleeping bag and placed her extra blanket around her shoulders. The chill that had accompanied the Wendigo's appearance had not left with it, and the campfire was still burning low.

He retrieved a couple of the seed pods from his bag. Punching holes in them as before, he placed them near the fire, and once again the escaping gas fed the flames, causing them to blaze up into life again.

Errol stared at the flames, debating his options. Digby had said that the Wendigo chose one victim per night. He would have to watch Gale carefully, as it was clear that she was next on its list. Even as the thought occurred to him, he saw her get up and start walking as if to exit the camp. He raced to her, turning her around and leading her back, but it was clear that she was not in her

86

right mind. It would take extreme vigilance to make sure she did not end up in the monster's gullet tonight. And even if she didn't, his own number would be up the following night. In short, this was likely the last night for both of them unless they found a way to fight the thing hunting them.

He put Gale into her sleeping bag and cinched it up. She just lay there, staring up at the nighttime sky and muttering to herself. Errol moved away and went to place another seed pod near the fire. They needed a plan (although using the term "they" was a misnomer at this point, as it was clear Gale would be of no help). As he watched the hissing gas escape, he thought back on the seed pod Gale had tossed on the fire earlier, and how they had laughed about it afterwards.

And that will probably be the last thing I'll ever laugh about. My last bit of fun is exploding seed.

And with that notion, a sudden thought occurred to him. He turned it over in his mind, working the pros and cons of it, trying to figure out if there were any other options, until he finally decided that it was the only course of action under the circumstances.

Why not? Might as well go out with a bang.

Decision made, he went through his pack to retrieve the items that would make what he had to do easier. Then he went to Gale and climbed into her sleeping bag with her, adjusting it so that it covered them completely - even their heads.

****

The Wendigo, once again far from its prey, was still able to easily see the goings-on in the camp. It watched the boy crawl into the girl's sleeping bag with her, an act which was then followed by various movements in the sleeping bag itself.

The boy had given it a serious wound. Although it had begun healing immediately after the silver was removed, the injury was still painful. Moreover, the ache only exacerbated the Wendigo's already-insatiable hunger.

It thought that perhaps the girl would come tonight; she had succumbed to the Fever with extreme swiftness, and was practically begging to be devoured.

Regardless, whether she came tonight or not, it would end this hunt the next night.

Chapter 17

The next morning saw Errol more chipper than he had been in days. Everything had gone almost perfectly the night before. He didn't feel like a man who was possibly facing his last day; instead, he felt a calm sense of finality, as if he could now accept anything fate had in store for him.

He glanced at Gale. She looked as though she had gotten no sleep at all, and that was very much the case. After he had finished in her sleeping bag, he had gone back to his own. However, before sleep claimed him, he twice had to get up and stop her from wandering off. After the second time, he had settled for binding her hands and feet with a length of rope from his saddle.

Upon waking, he had untied her, but she still had a vacant look in her eyes and seemed unable to take note of anything going on around her. Rather than travel with her in this condition, Errol decided they would stay put and make their stand exactly where they were.

****

Unfortunately, the good spirits that Errol had awakened with did not appear to have much longevity. As the day wore on, his mood changed, becoming more fearful and hesitant. He vaguely wondered whether this was due to his own nature or the influence of the Wendigo - the Fever.

As twilight began to fall, he went about starting a campfire for the night. As he set ablaze the plants he had collected and carefully laid out earlier for their fire, he reviewed his plan again, less sure in the coming darkness as to whether or not it had even a chance of succeeding. He looked at Gale, who was - for all intents and purposes - still catatonic. She was sitting on a blanket, staring at the fire. He had tried moving her away several times, to keep her out of the danger that was to come, but she kept returning to the same spot. Finally, he had given up and settled for draping a thick blanket over her head and allowing it to hang down, covering much of her face.

He didn't bother with warding the camp this time, as doing so had proven to be only mildly effective against the Wendigo, and he might need every bit of power later. Moreover, even if wards had been able to stop it, they were of limited value when the monster's prey - in the clutch of Wendigo Fever - willingly left the protection they provided and offered themselves to the creature. No, he would not die like that; he'd rather die fighting, while he was still in his right mind.

Convinced that he had made the right decision, Errol looked to the horizon, where the setting sun slowly descended, a huge orange orb taking its warmth and protection with it as it continued to drop. As the last ray of light vanished, a chill wind blew into the camp. As it had the night before, the campfire diminished somewhat, and the horses neighed wildly, maddened with fright.

The Wendigo had arrived.

Chapter 18

As always, the monster had simply appeared as if out of thin air. The wound that the silver had made in its stomach was almost completely healed, the only evidence of what had happened being an angry patch of newly-formed, reddish skin in the place where the dart had landed.

This time, the Wendigo didn't stand still but strode across the camp, towards Gale.

"No!" Errol shouted. "Me first!" He had his axe in his hand and dropped into a low fighting stance. The Wendigo made an odd noise, like something between a cough and growl. It took Errol a second to realize that the thing was laughing. Regardless, it seemed to accept his challenge, because it strode over to where he was and stood towering over him.

Errol moved forward, swinging in a left-to-right arc at the monster's midsection (which was about the height of Errol's head). It lithely stepped aside; following the axe's momentum, Errol spun in a circle and swung at the creature again. Once more, it avoided the blow with ease.

Staying low, Errol circled, apparently looking for an opening but - more importantly - trying to get properly situated with respect to his plan. The Wendigo circled with him. When it was in the position that Errol wanted – between him and the campfire, with its back to the flames (and with Gale on the opposite side of the blaze) – Errol charged straight at it. He brought the axe up for an overhand strike in his right hand and swung as hard as he could.

The Wendigo caught the blade in its claw. At the same time that it did so, Errol – with his left hand – tossed a seed pod between the thing's legs and into the campfire.

Errol released his axe into the monster's grip and fell back, covering his face as the gas-filled pod exploded, spewing its contents in all directions. For the second time in as many nights, Errol heard the Wendigo scream in pain. It dropped the axe and spun around, still wailing, while reaching over its shoulder with one claw and behind its back with another, trying to get at something.

As it turned its back towards him, Errol witnessed a sight that gave him courage. The Wendigo had several great, weeping wounds on its backside, from its shoulders all the way down to its calves. It was as if its flesh was made of ice and was now melting due to some internal fire.

It's working! It's working!

Errol's plan was basically very simple. He had taken the pure silver links from the revenant's bracelet and – using his knife – had cut them up into smaller bits. He had then punctured the seed pods, and followed this up with pushing the silver bits inside. Finally, he had sealed the little holes in the pods with the epoxy from his medicine kit. The result was seed pods that would still inflate (or blow up), but with a little something extra inside.

All of this he had done while in Gale's sleeping bag with her. He had dared not do it in the open for fear that the monster would see him, and a lot of activity by him – in his sleeping bag alone – might also make it wary. He was far more willing to let it think whatever it wanted about his activities in Gale's sleeping bag while he brought his plan to fruition.

Everything had worked as he had hoped, with the pod exploding and shredding the Wendigo with silver shrapnel. Errol's joy at success, however, was short-lived. In what was almost a sickening act, Errol saw the thing thrust its claws into its own chest - much like the night before - and then dig around before coming out with something: a bit of silver! In essence, the creature – unable to get at the silver from the entry points in its back – was, in a remarkable act of self-preservation, digging the metal out through the front of its body.

Errol was so shocked that, for a second, he couldn't move. However, by the time the creature had pulled out a second piece of silver, he was in motion. He ran forward and scooped up his axe, then swung with all his might at the Wendigo's right knee. It was like striking a stone, but flesh and tendon came apart as the blow connected.

Already weak from the infiltration of silver, the leg collapsed under the additional damage caused by the axe, and the Wendigo went down on one knee with a shriek. Still screaming, it swatted at Errol, connecting with a backhand that sent him flying.

The impact when he hit the ground knocked the breath out of him, and he lay there dazed for a moment. He looked at the Wendigo, saw that it was still mining silver from its chest, and struggled to his feet. He pulled another seed pod from his pocket and flung it towards the campfire. Shockingly, the Wendigo reached for it with a claw that was bloody and slick with its own gore.

Errol bit his knuckle in anguish as the monster seemed to snag the pod. However, it actually missed, although it did indeed make contact with the pod, throwing its trajectory off. It hit the ground a few feet shy of the fire. The Wendigo looked at Errol, making its weird laugh again, and continued removing the silver bits from its body. Errol made as if to circle around, but the monster, despite its collapsed knee, scrambled along the ground to keep itself between him and the pod. Errol, forgetting about his warding wand, held up his right hand and uttered an incantation. He curled the hand into a fist as a hazy blue-white glow began forming around it.

Suddenly, the campfire flared up, the result of Errol having carefully laid the firewood (or rather, the plants he was using as firewood) in the pattern of a ward earlier. The Wendigo turned to look at it just as the heat made the pod Errol had thrown explode. It sent a second load of silver projectiles flying at the creature. The monster howled and clutched at its face, neck, and chest. When it turned back to Errol, he could see that its face was a ruin. One eye was gone, leaving nothing but a sickly yellow socket. Its nose and cheeks had been shredded, leaving strips of skin hanging down like melting globs of goo. Likewise, its torso was peppered with holes where fragments of silver had entered, making Errol wonder how it was still holding together in one piece.

Errol held out his hand and fired a spark from his palm. It struck the Wendigo in the chest and knocked it back into the campfire, which suddenly blazed up around the creature in an eerie black flame that Errol had never seen or heard of before. The monster got up, coated in ebony flames and shrieking like a banshee, so loud, prolonged, and blood-chilling that Errol had to cover his ears. Then it collapsed back down into the fire, which continued burning black around the body.

Taking a deep breath, Errol flopped to the ground in exhaustion.

It's over.

He looked towards Gale, hoping that the blanket had protected her when the seed pods exploded - and experienced a mild moment of panic when he didn't see her. He stood up and looked around wildly. She was gone.

"Gale!" he called out desperately. "Gale!"

She must have slipped away while he was fighting the Wendigo. What would killing the Wendigo do as far as the Fever? Was she still under some weird compulsion?

He studied the area where she had been sitting, and saw her tracks leading off into the marsh. He held up his wand, letting its light flare brightly against the gloomy darkness. He was about to follow after her when he heard something behind him. Thinking it was her, he braced himself to turn, only to have something hard and solid connect with the back of his head before he could do so.

Chapter 19

He was tied up when he came to, his arms firmly bound behind him. He heard an odd undulating chant as he opened his eyes and looked around. He was still at the fire marsh campsite. The chanting stopped.

"You're awake," said a vaguely familiar voice. Errol looked in the direction that it came from. His vision was a little blurry, but he blinked a few times and things slowly came into focus.

"Jarruse!" Errol exclaimed. "What are you doing here?"

"Just reclaiming what was rightfully mine," the man said, tapping something next to him. He stood over by the campfire, which was almost out now. Looking closely, Errol could see the monstrous skeleton of the Wendigo in the dying embers; shockingly, the skeleton had turned completely black. Errol also recognized the item that Jarruse had tapped: the odd book of magic from Tom's pack.

"I have to say, you Magnuses are incredible examples of manhood," Jarruse continued. "I was impressed when I saw your brother escape from the Wendigo, but you! Actually *killing* one! I've never even heard of such a thing. Hell, I hadn't even known escape was possible until Tom."

Tom was alive???!!!

"What happened to him?"

"The Wendigo, of course. It chased him from the cabin, through the marsh here, to some fields nearby."

"Then what?"

Jarruse chuckled. "A roc. That's what happened."

"A rock? Like a boulder?" Errol was perplexed.

"A *roc*. A giant bird. It dropped out of the sky, grabbed your brother's horse and flew away with it. He had tied himself to the horse, so it flew away with him, too. The Wendigo was furious."

"So my brother got lucky?"

"I'm not sure luck had anything to do with that roc showing up. I think your brother summoned it."

Of course! Tom had that ability!

"Why would you say that?" Errol asked anyway.

"Because I'm a sorcerer, and I felt magic in the air before it happened."

"A sorcerer?" This was worse than Errol thought.

"Yes. The *supreme* sorcerer now that I have this." Again, he tapped the book.

"What is that exactly?"

Jarruse laughed. "The consummate book of magic. It belonged to my great-great-grandfather." He mumbled something, then brought an axe down on the Wendigo skeleton, chopping an arm free of the remains.

"Unfortunately," he continued, "although he was an extremely powerful sorcerer, Great-great-grandfather was also a bit of a do-gooder. So, it was only natural that he would get involved when he heard about some unstoppable monster terrorizing this region and eating people."

"The Wendigo."

"Yes. But even with the power of the book, he wasn't able to kill the thing. The best he could do was put it to sleep, make it hibernate forever. So that's what he did, and he put a spell on the Wendigo's cabin to make it impossible to find. But there was a price: the book had to stay with the monster to keep the magic effective."

"So you came back for it, took the book, and woke the Wendigo up."

"Not exactly," Jarruse retorted, as he continued dissecting the skeleton. "I didn't lie when I said I'd hired some men to come here with me to retrieve some items for my work. But yes, after I broke the spell hiding the cabin, I sent them into it – the Wendigo's lair – to get the book, and in doing so they woke up the Wendigo." Jarruse chuckled. "I suppose they would have had a better chance if I'd told them what would happen."

"So, they took the book, then it woke up and killed them?"

"It's more like they *disturbed* the book, woke it up, and it killed them. Which compounded my problem, but that's where your brother came in."

"My brother? You set him up to be killed by that monster?!"

Jarruse seemed to consider for a moment, but answered honestly. "Yes, but I've caused the deaths of dozens in my quest for the book; what was one more? I had hoped that - after he found its lair - the Wendigo would leave to pursue him, which would allow me to enter the cabin and get the book."

"Except Tom found it and took it with him."

"Yes."

"How did the Wendigo get Tom's pack?"

"It wasn't far away when the roc swooped down to grab him. Wendigos are fast, and it raced into the field after him. It leaped at your brother, trying to snatch him back down, but only managed to get a grip on his pack, which he let drop. It took the pack – with the book in it – back to the cabin, putting me back at square one."

"And that's when you sent me in, hoping like before that the Wendigo would pursue me and leave you to get the book from the cabin. Except this time, I took it with me."

"Yes."

"And how is it that, through all this, you managed to avoid getting killed by the Wendigo yourself?"

Jarruse touched one of the bracelets on his wrist. "This charm helps shield my presence from predators like that. As long as I didn't come into direct conflict with the Wendigo, the charm's magic made it ignore me. So all I've had to do is sit back and watch, waiting for my chance."

Errol became silent as Jarruse continued hacking up the skeleton. After a few moments, he asked, "What are you doing with the Wendigo remains?"

"In actuality, powerful weapons can be forged from the bones of a Wendigo - arrowheads that can pierce anything, blades that never dull - but you only have a limited amount of time to make them. You see, burning the body was the right idea – it makes it harder for the Wendigo to resurrect – but it also turns the skeleton black. After the bones cool, they will harden to such an extent that they will be almost impervious, so you have to chop the skeleton up and forge your weapons before that happens."

"Which is what you are doing now."

"Yes. Now be silent so I can finish, or I'll cut out your tongue."

****

99

Over the next two hours, Errol sat in total silence while Jarruse chanted and read from his book, performing dark magic that warped the Wendigo bones and shaped them into various armaments and weapons. He struggled to free himself, but to no avail; he was solidly bound. Forgetting his own fate for a moment, he looked around for Gale, but she was still nowhere to be seen. He had been tempted to ask Jarruse about her, but now he was happy that he had been ordered to be silent; maybe the sorcerer had forgotten about her, meaning there was still a chance that she could survive all this.

As to his own fate, Errol had no doubt as to what would happen. The only thing that had kept him alive was that Jarruse was on a very tight time frame with respect to the Wendigo bones.

At last, the sorcerer let out a weary breath. He seemed exhausted by his efforts, as he should have been. The black magics have a tendency to suck out pieces of your life, your soul. Small wonder then that Jarruse's conscience was unbothered by the thought of all the men he had sent to their deaths.

"You're done, I take it?" Errol asked.

"Yes," Jarruse answered, holding up an odd dagger to the light. It was all black, but seemed to be inlaid with streaks of silver along the handle and the blade. "Unfortunately, the end of this effort for me also means the end of life for you." He gripped the blade and came at Errol.

Suddenly, something whizzed by the sorcerer's head, so close that it left a bloody scrape from his right temple to the back of his skull. Errol recognized it immediately as a bolt from his one-hand crossbow.

Jarruse froze, looking intently in the direction the shot had come from.

"Don't move," said a voice that, just a few days earlier, Errol would have sworn he preferred never to hear. "Stay right where you are, or the next one is through your heart."

Standing still, Jarruse raised his hands, and suddenly Gale was there, striding forth with the crossbow aimed – as she had mentioned – at his chest. She also had Errol's pack slung over her shoulder.

"Drop the dagger," she said, and like a smart man, Jarruse complied. "Now, come over here and untie him."

Jarruse came forward as directed. Gale tried to back up, to keep distance between her and the man, but she slipped. Jarruse took advantage of the opportunity to rush her. He tackled her hard, and they both went down, the crossbow firing wildly to one side. Errol's pack popped open, and its contents spilled along the ground.

Jarruse, being stronger, wrestled himself on top of Gale, then pinned her arms with his legs. He pulled back a meaty fist, preparing to hit her, when a strange look came over his face. He opened up his fist, and Errol noted that he was holding the gemstone from the revenant bracelet. The soulgate.

The sorcerer cast it aside in anger, then pulled back again to hit Gale. As before, however, the expression on his face changed, and when he opened up the same fist again, the gemstone was there once more.

Something in Jarruse must have recognized the jewel for what it was, because he gasped as he stared at it, then flung it away again. But when he looked at his palm a third time, the gemstone was back again. At that point, Jarruse screamed.

101

At the same time, the air behind Jarruse began to shimmer and glow, taking on the vague semblance of a man as the revenant appeared. The sorcerer seemed to sense it behind him and turned, scrambling to his feet and whimpering.

"No, no," Jarruse muttered, almost inaudibly. "Please, no…"

"Revenge!" said the revenant. "Death! Revenge! Death!" Apparently it was one of the many who had met their demise at the hands of the sorcerer.

It closed in on Jarruse as he backed away, pleading. Now Errol knew why the revenant had materialized on the Beverly farm, what the connection was. Somehow, it had known that Gale and Errol would cross paths with Jarruse - the person responsible for its death.

"Gale!" Errol shouted, as the revenant shot towards the sorcerer. "Don't look!"

Errol shut his own eyes, but couldn't block out the terrifying screams, or the nauseating, wet sounds of slaughter that took place just a few feet from him.

It felt like a long time, but he kept his eyes squinted shut until he felt hands tugging at the ropes that bound him. He rubbed his hands as they came free, trying to improve circulation. Then he did something that was probably a shock to Gale - who had untied him - as well as himself. He gave a long, lingering hug to one of the Beverly women.

WARDEN: BOOK 1

Chapter 20

He escorted Gale back to her family's farm. By
the time they arrived, she had essentially recovered from
the effects of the Wendigo Fever. Apparently, while he
had been battling the monster, its hold on her had – for
reasons unknown - compelled her to leave the campsite.
By the time she found her way back, Errol was in the
hands of the sorcerer. However, while Jarruse was
preoccupied with his weapon-making, she had been able
to get her hands on Errol's pack and weapons.

As to the Wendigo weapons themselves, there
were ten arrowheads made from the monster's claws, the
silver-inlaid dagger, and a few other blades. Errol debated,
but decided to keep them when he realized that they were
indeed powerful arms. (He also decided to keep Jarruse's
book of magic, as well as the sorcerer's charms and
personal effects, although retrieving everything after the
man's death had been a grisly affair.)

Aware of the fact that Wendigos can occasionally
resurrect themselves, Errol had spread the creature's
remaining bones far and wide. Knowing flame to be one
of the monster's weaknesses, he buried a number of the
bones randomly around the fire marsh. He put a
compulsion on an eagle to fly several to faraway regions,
dropping them over land and sea. He buried many in out-
of-the way places, adhering silver to them with the epoxy.
He even left one of its bones at the site of the Wendigo's
cabin (which he burned to the ground, along with all the
human remains he found in the area). In short, Errol
found various ways to get rid of the monster's remnants.

The only item that he took special care with was
the creature's skull. That he placed in a jar with silver and

103

buried beneath the Station House porch. It was unlikely that the monster could be resurrected without its head, and if the creature ever came for it, the Wendigo wouldn't be able to take possession of the skull without the Warden being aware of it.

****

Errol sat on the Station House porch his first day back, watching the sun go down. To say the past few days had been difficult would be a major understatement. That he had survived was essentially a miracle, but nothing that he himself could take credit for. Everything that he had accomplished had been because of his brother Tom. Tom's teaching. Tom's training. Tom's words of wisdom. Tom had saved his life without even being there.

Moreover, Tom was somewhere out there, alive. Tom would never have given up on him, so Errol knew he'd never give up on Tom. He'd keep searching until he found his brother, alive or dead. In the meantime, he would honor Tom's memory, Tom's legacy, here in Stanchion Ward.

Errol looked down at the piece of paper in his hand. He had retrieved it from a raven just a few minutes earlier. It came from the Pierce farm and read:

STRANGE ANIMAL ATTACKING CATTLE

Errol scribbled out a message and sent a bird back with it, saying he would be there first thing in the morning.

65382125R00069

Made in the USA
Lexington, KY
10 July 2017